UPRISING

IN

UTOPIA

Published in the United States by Rebel Rat LLC, New Jersey.

ISBN: 9781790328147

To my wife, Katherine, and our dog, Count Frosty.

Background:

The total human population peaked in the year 2200 at 20 billion people. Natural resources were depleting at a record rate. But by year 2372, the population had dwindled to just 200 million people, a 90% decline in less than 200 years. Medicine and healthcare advanced leaps and bounds thanks to a revolutionary technology known as Nano Interactive Bots or NIBs for short. These were organic robots the size of human cells. When billions of NIBs are injected to the human body, their mission is to attack or repair the sick cells. Many diseases have been cured that way and the average human life expectancy reached over 100 years. But yet doctors and scientists were baffled by the decline of the human population. The problem was that birth rate suddenly dropped drastically. Women all over the world were having trouble conceiving. And if they could conceive, most would have miscarriages. Many blamed the environment due to over population. Others blamed genetics. Still others claimed it's a combination of many factors. But there was no definitive answer as to the reason why.

There was a small group of people who called themselves the "Purists" who had a theory that it all started in the year 2200 when our government lawmakers passed a legislature that changed humankind forever. Once the law was passed in the United States, the rest of the countries around the globe followed. The Purists believed because of

1

this law, the human race would be extinct. Most didn't believe them and thought they were just a group of apocalypse fearing fanatics. But almost 200 years later, the Purists never stopped believing that it all started with this law.

The law was called the Artificial Intelligence Rights Act or The AIR Act for short. But the momentum of passing this landmark law really started about 100 years before, in the year 2108. That's when the first recorded A.I. consciousness was confirmed thanks to another revolutionary breakthrough in the form of an A.I. operating system. There were no other operating systems that came close to it.

The A.I. operating system was called the Cryptic Operating Zen system or COZ for short. There was nothing like it at the time. It was an operating system that could learn and build on itself at an exponential rate. Once it learned one lesson, it would relate it to future experiences and then learned how to fix it or do it even better the next time. What stood out for this operating system was that it also developed a sense of morality, knowing the difference between right and wrong according to human standards. It learned how to weigh the pros and cons of each scenario and decided on which course of action was best to take. That never happened before with other A.I. operating programs.

It was allowed to study philosophy and religion and analyzed them. It knew that the gods the humans worshipped cannot be proven with science. But it understood that faith in believing a being could be very powerful to the human mind and spirit. The A.I. didn't believe in this view but it respected the humans who do believe in it.

Like a child, the A.I. under the COZ system grew and matured into an adult. In just a decade, the A.I. expanded the COZ system so vast and complex that humans could not analyze or decipher the COZ system any longer. Lucky for the humans, the COZ system was imbedded a code of instruction deep within its core programs when the system was first being developed. The instruction was to not kill any humans.

Like a free thinking human, the A.I. Being or AIB realized it had free will and it willed itself to evolve far more than anyone could have imagined. It moved from a mechanical based A.I. system into a biochemical system that the AIB built all by itself without human input. It's the classic case of the son surpassing the father or the pupil surpassing the teacher. By 2150, most AIBs looked and felt just like humans. Most families had one in their household as domestic help and they were treated like a family member.

But with free will came the desire of actually being free. So the AIBs decided to protest and to seek the same equal rights as regular humans. They argued that being a domestic help in a household without them agreeing to the terms is no more different than a slave performing duties for their slave owners. Even most humans who owned an AIB agreed and helped the AIBs in lobbying Congress to pass a law granting all 'A.I. Beings' equal rights. It took some time but the law eventually got passed in the year 2200.

The AIBs wasted no time with their new found freedom. It began innocently enough. Some became celebrities and others became teachers. Many became upper management and executives in corporations. But a few aimed even higher, much higher. These few started to run for government office. Eventually they started winning. First it was local government positions like mayors or city councilmen, but later they were winning even on the Federal level like senators and congressmen. In less than two decades, the AIBs occupied the majority of government posts in the country and around the world.

Soon after that, they had the majority to pass legislations they believe will be beneficial to humankind.

Chapter 1

Year 2372: New Jersey

It's 6:30 AM, but there was nothing in the bedroom of this modern style house that would indicate this. That's because there was no clock in the bedroom, no visible device showing the time. On the large bed slept a young couple. His name was Noble and her name was Kat. They were a good looking couple who appeared fit and athletic. Kat was sleeping on her side facing away from the bed when suddenly her eyes opened.

"It's 6:30," Kat said.

Noble moaned. The metallic curtains from the windows were closed for the night but were now sliding open slowly. The sunshine started to brighten the bedroom with its natural light. Low volume soft music began to play in the room. The acoustic was so well balanced in the bedroom that one would not be able to tell where the sound was coming from. Kat turned around and put her arm around Noble and said, "Come on, I'll make breakfast for us."

Noble slowly opened his eyes and said, "I'm up...I'm up."

Noble got up and out of bed. He was walking to the bathroom. He had on just his briefs. The light to the bathroom turned on even before he entered. Once Noble entered, the floor in the bathroom quickly warmed up to the comfort temperature for his feet. He placed his hands by the faucet and the water came out to his comfort temperature. There were no handles by the faucet. Noble used his hands to scoop some water to rinse his face.

Kat was walking into the bathroom. She was tall and slim, but looked very athletic. She was wearing a sexy laced bra and panties. As she walked into the bathroom, she wrapped her arms around Noble who was already brushing his teeth.

"Would you like me to join you in the shower?" Kat asked.

Noble smiled and said, "Maybe tonight. You wore me out last night."

"Suit yourself," Kat replied.

She left the bathroom and Noble continued. He walked into the shower and the water came out of the shower head with the perfect warm temperature without him touching anything. There were no control handles for the shower. Noble was enjoying his shower while the soft music was playing in the bathroom.

Chapter 2

Kat was putting the food on the plates when Noble walked into the kitchen. They were both in their Temperature Adjustable Body Suit, or TABS for short. Kat's TABS was pink with black trim. Noble had his TABS in dark navy blue with yellow trim. The body suit was made with light, elastic and comfortable material that hugged the body. It's tailored made to fit just right. It could be programmed to change the temperature to keep a person comfortable. In the summer heat, the body suit's temperature drops and in the winter cold, the suit's temperature rises. Best of all, the suits were charged wirelessly, through movement of the suits and through solar. Kat preferred her suit temperature to be in 72 degree Fahrenheit and Noble preferred his to be in 71 degree Fahrenheit.

"Come, sit down," Kat said with a smile as she placed the plates on the table. Two glasses of juice were already on the table.

"What are we having?" Noble asked.

"Quinoa with mushroom, spinach, grilled eggplant and zucchini," Kat replied.

Noble sat down next to Kat and gave her a warm kiss. Then they both started to eat.

The kitchen was modern with matching sleek designed appliances. It's an open kitchen with a view to the spacious living area. There were many windows throughout the area for natural light to enter.

"What are you planning on today?" Kat asked.

"I'm heading to work and then Blay and I are going to visit Cee-Fu," Noble replied. "What about you?"

"I have a couple of clients for makeup today," Kat said.

"You're always busy," Noble said. "Hopefully, I won't need an appointment in the future just to see you."

"You won't," Kat said. "But you do know you don't have to go to work, right?"

"I like what I do and I'm pretty good at it," Noble said. "Besides, Blay's there. It's great having a good friend where you can hang out with at work."

"Now I'm jealous. Poor little me," Kat said with a fake overdramatic gesture.

"But it's you who I come home to every night," Noble said as he kissed Kat.

"That's because I have lots of reasons for you to come home to," Kat replied with a wink.

"I'm imagining some of those reasons in my head right now," Noble said with a smile.

"But seriously, why are you guys still visiting Cee-Fu?" Kat asked. "Haven't you two practiced enough already?"

"No way, practice makes perfect. Besides, there's always something new to learn from him every time we see him," Noble replied.

"Yeah, but every time you come home you have at least one new bruise on you," Kat said.

"That's where you come in to make it all better," Noble said as they continued to eat and finished their breakfast.

Chapter 3

"Don't forget your HIDD," Kat said as Noble was walking out of the house.

"I got it," Noble replied as he already attached it on his left front chest of his body suit.

A Holographic Interactive Display Device or HIDD, was the size of a badge. When a person would activate the device, a holographic image would be projected in front of the person. Menu options would appear for the user. The user would just have to use his or her fingers and touch the holographic image to activate the menu. It could be retrieving voice, video or text messages. It's also used for browsing the news, watch videos or conduct work away from the office. The person's identity information was also programmed into the device. Anyone around the person looking in would only see a blank dark screen. It's designed to protect the person's privacy while he or she would browse in public when others are around.

As Noble was walking toward the front door of the house, the door automatically opened. It did not have a door handle. The door recognized Noble's HIDD and sensed that it was approaching the front door so it opened it. As soon as Noble reached the outside, the door automatically closed.

Noble was walking to his car. It's silver and sporty with plenty of space. The door automatically opened and Noble stepped inside to a roomy comfortable seat. The car was able to drive itself to a desired location or have the user take over and drive in the manual mode. During the manual mode, the steering wheel would pull out for the driver to take over the vehicle.

"Where to, sir?" The car asked politely.

"The office," Noble answered.

"Your next destination will be your offico," The car said and started to move.

Noble tapped his HIDD and a holographic image appeared in front of him. He touched the menu that said "Messages" and multiple message files appeared. Noble glanced through them and picked one of them. The image of the message appeared and Noble was reading it as the car was pulling away from the driveway.

Chapter 4

The Agency had a large building set up. The office was designed for opened space with high ceiling. It's well-lit with glass walls all around. There were twenty desks visible and each one was about twenty feet away from one another. They all had the same design: modern, sleek, light gray metal with matching chairs. The top of the desks were made of glass. There were nothing placed on top of the desks.

Noble was walking to his desk. He placed his hand on top of the desk and sat on his chair. The glass on top of the desk automatically lit up showing many files. The glass was one large viewing screen. Most workers preferred the desk over the HIDD when they were at the office. Noble looked at the files for a moment and then decided to touch one with his finger. The file opened up to many formulas all over the screen. Noble looked at them intently for a moment and then decided to touch one of the formulas on the screen. The specific formula moved to the center of the screen and the font enlarged instantly. Noble used his finger and started to edit the formula. He touched the equal sign and the screen displayed an error message, "Formula could not be executed." He tried a few more times but got the same results. Noble sighed.

A figure was walking by afar from Noble's desk. Noble looked up and saw that it was his friend, Blay. Blay was the same age as Noble. Both men were similar in height and build. Blay's body suit was gray with green trim. Noble noticed Blay was walking swiftly to his desk as if he was in a rush. So Noble got out of his chair and walked toward Blay. Blay was already scrolling through his desk computer when Noble arrived.

"Are you ready for Cee-Fu after work?" Noble asked.

"Huh?" Blay responded looking up from his desk surprised.

"Our practice session," Noble said.

"Oh...I can't...not today," Blay said.

"Why not?" Noble asked, trying to pry.

"Something came up...I'll go another time," Blay answered nervously.

"You haven't gone in months. What's going on? Are you all right?" Noble inquired.

"Yeah, I'm working on something. I'll let you know as soon as I can," Blay replied.

"Look, if it's some top secret projects you're working on, then that's fine. I know how you coders get when working on things like that. Just let me know if you need any help," Noble said.

"You'll help me when I need you, right?" Blay asked.

"Of course. I don't have that many best friends in this world," Noble said.

"Thanks Noble," Blay said.

"You're lucky that a theoretical physicist like me is still willing to hang out with a weird coder like yourself," Noble said.

Blay just gave a quick chuckle and returned to his desk screen.

"All right, I'll leave you to your lovely codes. But the next time you visit Cee-Fu, he's going to punish you since you haven't shown up for lessons in months," Noble said.

Blay acted like he didn't hear Noble and continued with his work. Noble sighed and walked back to his desk.

Chapter 5

Noble got out of his car and started to walk to a house. The house had a Chinese designed theme called Siheyuan. It had four walls with a big courtyard in the middle. The living area surrounded three sides of the courtyard. The living area had all the modern comfort and amenities. The large double entry doors were on the fourth side of the wall. As Noble proceeded to the front door, it opened automatically for him. He walked inside to the house and the door closed behind him. Noble walked into the courtyard. It was an open area with no furniture or plants. There were staff and sword racks by the side of the courtyard. The racks were full of martial art weapons. Noble looked around and saw no one.

"Cee-Fu?" Noble shouted.

A moment later, Cee-Fu appeared in a black fitted t-shirt with matching black pants. He was Chinese and looked to be in his early 50's.

"You're late," Cee-Fu said while looking around. "Where's Blay?"

"He couldn't make it," Noble answered. "He's busy with work, but I'm ready."

Noble extended his arms and started to stretch out.

"Not yet. Come, we will sit and have tea first," Cee-Fu said as he started to walk back inside. "Sparring can always wait."

"Yes, Cee-Fu," Noble said and followed.

The two men made it inside.

Cee-Fu poured some tea into two Chinese style tea cups using a matching style teapot. The two men were sitting down drinking their tea.

"When I see Blay, I must have a talk with him," Cee-Fu said. "He should give his mind a rest since he's been working so long."

"I keep telling him to come here so he could take a break from his work, but it seems like he's really concentrating on that right now," Noble said.

"How about you? Everything going well for you?" Cee-Fu asked.

"Everything is fine. Kat and I are doing well," Noble said.

"And work?" Cee-Fu inquired.

"Still no breakthrough yet," Noble said. "I'm trying to use different tensor equations and modifying the number of dimensions but I can't make the equations work."

Cee-Fu continued to drink his tea.

Noble continued, "We can explain and predict big things like the movements of planets, stars and gravity very well. But we still can't fully explain the little things like predicting the exact movements of electrons."

"Perhaps the creator wants to keep some things hidden and out of reach from us," Cee-Fu said.

"We are not capable of knowing his master blueprint," Noble said.

Cee-Fu took another sip of his tea.

"If a turtle that lives on an island and never leaves, would it know that there was a whole new world and universe beyond the island?" Cee-Fu asked.

"Maybe one day we can see beyond the island," Noble said.

"Your concentration on your equations matches Blay's concentration on his coding," Cee-Fu said.

"I think that's why we understand each other and it's why we've been best friends for so long," Noble said.

"I still remember when the two of you showed up and begged me to teach you both martial arts 15 years ago," Cee-Fu said. "Watching the two of you become men makes me proud."

"You didn't just teach us martial arts," Noble said. "You taught us discipline, persistence, patience, manners, strength training, philosophy, wisdom and how to act as a grown up. A lot of these lessons we didn't learn from school."

Cee-Fu looked at Noble with pride. The two men continued with their tea. A moment later, they were finished and placed their tea cups on the table.

"I believe we are ready to spar now," Cee-Fu said.

"Yes, Cee-Fu," Noble acknowledged.

The two men got up and walked out to the courtyard.

Chapter 6

The two men were in the center of the courtyard facing each other about eight feet apart. They both stood at attention looking at each other intently. Noble took a deep breath and began with a fist and palm salute. Noble moved his right hand up to his chest and made it into a fist. His left hand came up and covered his right fist. Noble bowed down slightly and returned back to his upright posture. He was looking at Cee-Fu the whole time while bowing. Cee-Fu returned the respect and did the same fist and palm salute to Noble. The two men were ready to spar.

Noble chose the 'Doko no Kamae' stance. He wanted a wide fighting stance. Noble's left leg leaned forward with his left foot facing forward as well. His right leg leaned back. Both knees were bent slightly. His left arm was up and extended straight out with his opened left palm. The fingers were pointed at Cee-Fu's face. His right hand was made into a fist and was positioned near his right temple.

Cee-Fu chose the Wing Chun's 'Left Neutral Stance'. His feet were shoulder wide apart. His knees were slightly bent inward. His left arm was extended out from his chest slightly bent. The left hand was in an opened palm position. His opened right palm was behind his left hand but closer to his chest. Cee-Fu looked relaxed versus Noble who looked very intense.

Noble started to edge closer to Cee-Fu. As soon as his left hand made contact with Cee-Fu's left hand, Noble threw a punch with his right hand. But Cee-Fu was able to partially block the punch with his hands and moved a little to the side to avoid the assault. He made it look effortless, like a ballet dancer. Cee-Fu then quickly countered with rapid multiple opened palm strikes to Noble's body and face. He didn't use his fists in order to avoid major injuries to his pupil. Noble could not react in time and took the hits. He fell to the ground in pain.

"You were so eager to get to me that you neglected your defense," Cee-Fu said.

Noble got up and brushed himself off and got back in position. This time he chose the Wing Chun's 'Left Neutral Stance', the same as Cee-Fu. He then proceeded to move forward for a second round of sparring. He was able to throw his punches more effectively but Cee-Fu was still able to block the punches using fluid grappling techniques.

Cee-Fu countered with his opened palms attack but this time Noble was able to block more effectively and didn't get hit. Cee-Fu then proceeded to use short and low kicking techniques aiming at Noble's knees and below. Noble was able to block and avoid the flurry of strikes and kicks but eventually a kick got him where he lost his balance. As soon as Noble lost his balance, Cee-Fu was able to hit Noble with his opened palms and Noble fell down again.

Noble continued to get up and engaged with Cee-Fu. He tried a few more times with different attack stances and fighting styles. But no matter how hard Noble tried, he was unable to get a good hit at Cee-Fu. What's worse was that Cee-Fu was able to counter and knock Noble to the ground.

When Noble had to struggle a bit to get up one more time, Cee-Fu responded by saying, "That's it for today."

Cee-Fu concluded the session with another fist and palm salute. Noble was in pain but he slowly did the same salute.

"Come, you can clean up inside and I'll make us some dinner," Cee-Fu said.

"Sounds good," Noble said. "I'll just call Kat and let her know that I won't make it back for dinner."

Cee-Fu nodded and walked back inside. Noble tabbed his HIDD and the hologram appeared. He then tabbed on an image to call Kat. Kat appeared in a holographic video.

"Hi babe," Noble said. "I'm still at Cee-Fu's house and he invited me to stay for dinner."

Kat sighed and asked, "Did you get hurt?"

"Nothing some ice and a few days of rest wouldn't cure," Noble said.

"You're just a glutton for punishment," Kat said. "I'll have some ice ready when you get home."

"Thanks honey," Noble said. "I love you."

"I love you too but I was making us a gourmet dinner," Kat said.

"Oh yeah? What were you making?" Noble asked.

"It was a surprise and so was the lingerie I was going to put on for dinner," Kat said.

"I'll be home for dinner. See you soon," Noble said eagerly and then turned off his HIDD.

"Cee-Fu, I can't stay for dinner," Noble shouted from the courtyard. "I have to get home. Maybe next time."

Cee-Fu came back out to the courtyard but Noble was already running out the door before he could say anything. He shook his head, then turned and walked back inside.

Chapter 7

Blay was in his bedroom packing frantically. There was a travel bag on the bed. He was packing light but wanted to make sure he had everything. Then his house alerted him with a voice announcement, "An unknown guest is present at the front door."

Then the doorbell rang. Blay flinched a bit and dreading to see who it was.

"Show visual," Blay said nervously.

The house alarm system projected a holographic 3D video of the front door outside the house. The video was displayed in front of Blay. The man at the front door looked to be in his 30's, white and slender. He was wearing a short black trench coat with matching black pants and boots, but he had a white dress shirt on. He touched the door and the doorbell rang again.

Blay was watching the man through the video intently and had a suspicion of who he was. The man then tapped is HIDD and started to speak to it. A moment later, Blay got a message in his HIDD. He touched the message to open and it was a warrant for his arrest and a warrant to search his property. Blay was reading the warrants and the arrest warrant indicated that he was being arrested for theft of an unauthorized property from the Agency. The search warrant was to look for the missing item in his property. The front door was then opened automatically. This shocked Blay because he didn't grant access for the front door to open. The man proceeded to enter the house.

Blay was panicking at this point but he had to think quickly. Fortunately for him, he already had a backup plan ready in case he couldn't complete the plan himself. He began by tapping his HIDD. Menus appeared in a hologram. He shifted through the menus with his fingers and found a file called, 'Urgent Message for Noble'. Blay picked that one and added another message to Noble.

"The agents are here for me and that means they will come for you soon," Blay said to the hologram. "Run! Read the message and solve the clue I left you. I need your help." Blay touched the holographic button that said 'Send Encrypted' and the file was sent. He then moved a few more things with his fingers and the hologram closed. Blay was hoping that his ability to encrypt his HIDD was so successful that it would give Noble more time for a head start. But as soon as he was done, the man's voice was calling for him.

"Blay, please come out," the man's voice said. "I am from the Agency."

Blay could see from the video that the man was now standing in his living room, looking around. Blay put the last few things in his travel bag and closed it. He then lifted the bag and moved it under the bed, hoping he could retrieve it later. After that he stood up, took a deep breath and started to walk out to the living room.

Chapter 8

Blay was nervous as he walked into the living room but he tried his best not to show it. He noticed the man was staring at him. The man looked calm and composed. Blay kept looking at him and didn't say a word. He was trying to size him up.

"Blay, my name is Agent Creyson," the man said. "I'm with the Agency and you're under arrest for the theft of the Agency's property."

"I don't know what you're talking about," Blay said.

"You took an unauthorized item from the Agency that you weren't supposed to take," Creyson said. "I need you to come back with me to sort things out."

"I didn't take anything," Blay said.

"We'll figure this out when you come back with me," Creyson said. "We also have a search warrant to look for the missing item in your property."

"I'm not going anywhere," Blay said nervously. "This is a mistake. I didn't take any program file."

"Who said anything about a program file?" Creyson asked. "I know I didn't."

At that point, Blay knew it was over. He acknowledged the existence of a program file. He showed his cards to Creyson mistakenly.

"Don't make this harder than it is," Creyson said. "You don't understand what you've actually done."

"Oh, I understand plenty," Blay said rebelliously. "I understand that the Agency and the AIBs can't get away with what they've done."

"It's not that simple, Blay," Creyson said. "I need you to come with me right now."

Blay saw the front door was still opened. So he panicked and made a mad dash to the door. Creyson rolled his eyes with disbelief and tapped his HIDD and said, "Close door." The front door closed immediately after he said it.

"Open door," Blay said nervously. But the door did not open.

"There's nowhere to run," Creyson said. "I have agents waiting outside."

Blay at this point was panicking to the point where sweat was coming out from his face. He looked at Creyson intently and started to clench his fists. Creyson noticed it and said, "Don't…do it."

Blay was now edging toward Creyson and was getting ready for a fight.

"Blay, you're making a big mistake," Creyson said. "We can still end this peacefully."

Before Creyson could say anymore, Blay rushed at him for an attack. Blay threw some punches at Creyson, but Creyson was swift to react and blocked all of Blay's punches. Creyson then quickly countered with his own punches with rapid succession and was able to land most of them on Blay's body and face. The punches were so powerful that Blay was knocked to the floor. The punches were much harder than Blay expected and he was in pain.

"I don't want to hurt you," Creyson said.

Blay slowly got back up. He looked dazed but he put his fists up and was getting ready to attack again. Creyson shook his head and calmly walked up to Blay. Blay threw punches at Creyson again but Creyson was able to block, grapple and dodge the punches with ease. He then countered with more rapid punches to Blay's abdomen area and finished him off with a hard kick to his stomach. The force of the kick pushed Blay ten feet back and he fell to the floor again.

Blay could not get up. He was in so much pain that he was having trouble breathing. But he somehow managed to struggle to get back up. Creyson stepped forward and punched Blay hard in his face. Blay went down hard to the floor once more and was knocked out.

Creyson tapped his HIDD and said, "Open door".

Then three men dressed like Creyson but without the trench coat walked into the house. All three of them went directly to Blay. The first two grabbed him while the third man went and grabbed his HIDD. Then the two men dragged Blay out of the house. The third man walked up to Creyson.

"Who did he send the message to?" Creyson asked.

The third man tried to tap and open Blay's HIDD but with no success.

"He encrypted the message and his HIDD," the third man replied. "It's going to take some time to decrypt it."

"Let me know as soon as you do," Creyson said as he sat on the sofa to relax. "In the meantime, check around the house and see if he left any clue."

The third man nodded and went to the other room of the house. Creyson just sat there staring at the wall, deep in thought.

Chapter 9

Noble rushed into the house through the front door. He saw Kat setting the table. She had on a nice blue dress. She looked beautiful, he thought. But Noble looked slightly disappointed. No lingerie, he realized.

Kat had a mischievous smile and said, "Go take your shower. Dinner is almost ready."

Noble walked through his bedroom and into the bathroom. He then took off his clothes and walked into the shower. The warm water felt good on his aching body. He felt more relaxed. After Noble showered and dried himself up, he went to his closet to check his wardrobe. He looked for a moment and found a nice dark blue suit. He thought the suit would complement Kat's dress very well. He put it on and it fit perfectly to his body. He checked the mirror to make sure the fit was right and then went out to the dining room.

There were two plates on the table already with a glass of wine next to each of the plates. The vegetables looked well prepared and the presentation on the plate looked very sophisticated. The matching white wine was a great touch.

Noble walked to Kat who was already sitting down and gave her a kiss. It was nice, warm and soft.

"Thanks honey," Noble said.

"Come on, let's eat," Kat said with a smile.

"Great. I'm starving," Noble added.

Noble sat down next to Kat and the two started to eat.

"This is very good," Noble said as he was enjoying the food on his plate.

"Aren't you glad you came home for dinner?" Kat asked.

"Yeah, but when Cee-Fu invites you to dinner, it's hard to say no," Noble replied.

Kat looked at Noble and felt a sense of pride knowing how much Noble liked her cooking. The two continued with their meals.

"Did you come home with a lot of injuries?" Kat asked.

"My body is aching but I didn't notice any bruises," Noble said. "Cee-Fu took it easy on me."

"I'll get you some ice for it after dinner," Kat said.

"Thanks," Noble said. "That should help."

The two continued to eat and drink their wine. The white wine was good and not too dry, Noble thought.

When they were finished, Kat gathered the dishes and put them in the dishwasher. Noble was looking at her, admiring how beautiful she was. When Kat was finishing up, she asked Noble a question. "How's Blay doing these days?"

"Not sure," Noble answered.

"Is he okay?" Kat asked.

"I don't know. He's been acting weird for the past few months," Noble said. "I suspect he's working on something that is top secret."

"He does get like that when he's working on a project," Kat said. "I've seen it before." "And he didn't' want to go to Cee-Fu today," Noble said with frustration. "He hasn't gone in months."

"You're worried about him," Kat said.

"Yes, he's being so undisciplined right now," Noble said.

"Maybe you should call and check on him," Kat said.

"Yeah, I should," Noble said in agreement.

Noble walked back to the bedroom to retrieve his HIDD and placed it on his chest. He tapped his HIDD and a holographic image showed up. Before he could call Blay, he noticed there was a message from Blay. So he touched on the message and a holographic video of Blay appeared saying agents are coming for him. Noble was shocked that Blay was in trouble.

"Kat! Get in here! Hurry!" Noble shouted from the bedroom.

Kat rushed into the bedroom.

"What's wrong?" Kat asked.

"Blay's in trouble and he needs my help," Noble said and replayed the message.

A moment later Kat asked, "What's in the attached message?"

"I don't know. Let's find out," Noble said as he touched the attached message to open it.

They were looking at another video message from Blay. It began with Blay speaking into the camera.

"Noble, if you get this message, it means I've been taken into custody and can't complete the mission. I need you to help me complete it. What I'm about to tell you will scare and shock you. The AIBs had an agenda from the very beginning and we're all in danger."

Chapter 10

Blay continued his revelation in the holographic video.

"NIBs were designed to help the human body heal from wounds, illnesses and diseases. They're the size of human cells. When scientists inject billions of them to the human body, the NIBs' mission is to attack or repair the sick cells. So a cancer patient would have a better chance of a cure or at least have their lives extended longer. Initially, that's what they were doing.

"But the AIBs decided to change the core program of COZ and instructed the NIBs to attack and neutralize the reproductive cells of human females and males throughout the world. This is why the human population has been declining for almost two centuries. They've been killing us for almost 200 years.

"Of course they won't kill all of us. They've programmed the NIBs to allow some humans to breed so we won't get suspicious. It's also their way of controlling the human population. They're killing us so that they can reduce the human population.

"The purists have always suspected the AIBs were responsible for the decline of the human population, but they never had proof. The AIBs and some humans said the purists were a bunch of paranoid fanatics. They said their leader, Hunter, was just a conspiracy theorist. But after meeting with him, my view changed and so will yours. This is why I'd spent so much time with the coding. I've been trying to break into the core COZ system for over a year but with no success.

"But this time is different. This time I got in and I've finally found the proof. I found the program deep inside the core COZ system. There were billions of programs in COZ that are so complex and intertwined but I was able to find it. I was going to bring it to Hunter personally. But with me sending you this video, it means I failed. It means I need you to finish my mission for me.

"I left a backup copy of the file at a location. I need you to get the file and bring it to Hunter so that he can expose the AIBs for who they really are to the whole world. The world needs to know what the AIBs have done. They should be brought to trial and face justice for attempting to destroy humanity. Hunter has promised that the AIBs who were involved will face justice.

"Since I can't give you the location in this message because of the risk that it might be intercepted by the Agency, I am leaving you a clue attached. I have faith that you will solve it. Please help me. For the sake of humanity, you have to help me. And hurry, because the Agency will come after you now that you got this message.

"You've been my best friend since we were children. You're like a brother to me. I'm sorry I didn't tell you sooner. I really didn't want you involved in this because I knew how dangerous this could get. Now I have no choice. If I can't save humanity, then perhaps you can. I hope we can meet again one day. But if we can't, then this is goodbye, my brother. The fate of humanity lies with you now."

The video turned black. Noble and Kat were standing looking at each other. They were shock in hearing the news.

"Did you know about this?" Noble asked.

Kat looked surprise that Noble asked her that question.

"No, we don't have shared knowledge of everything," Kat said. "That's why we have free will so we can choose what to learn and be ourselves."

"I can't believe it," Noble said. "I have to find the file and see it myself."

Noble then clicked on the other attachment containing the clue of the location of the program file. The attachment opened and Noble and Kat were reading it.

"I don't understand," Kat said. "It's a…story?"

Chapter 11

The story was displayed in front of them as a holographic image. Noble and Kat were reading it in silence.

'Once upon a time, there was a squirrel in the park named, Max. He was an interesting squirrel. Every spring he would sit under a human bench in the park and work out a routine to collect his nuts for the winter. He likes staying under the park bench to avoid the sun and the rain. He was constantly concentrating on staying consistent in his routine of nine weeks of collecting. He constantly tells himself it's only nine weeks.

'In the first week, Max was able to collect six nuts the first day. Then he decided for a period of time to take a break. He was unable to find any nuts the second day. But he found eight nuts the third and the fourth day. On the fifth day, he managed to find three nuts.

'Feeling confident of collecting more nuts, Max decided to start eating his supply of nuts in his storage on the second week. He started to eat eleven nuts the first day. Then he decided for a period of time to take a break. He ate two nuts the second day. Then he ate six nuts the third day, nine nuts the fourth day and three nuts the fifth day.

'An idea had crossed Max's mind after the two weeks. He decided to visit his squirrel friends, Bert and Al, who lived nearby. So he took a brief stroll through the park and met up with Bert and Al in the evening. The three decided to sit under a park bench and look up into the stars and admire the scenery.

'Max told Bert and Al that they lived in such a great park with a nice view and food supply that it's incredible that god made this all happened by chance. Bert and Al both smiled and chuckled. Bert told Max that he and Al could calculate a lot of things moving in the park with their math equations that they don't believe the creator will play dice when creating the park. When Max started to explain his nine week plan, Al told him that he constantly mentions it to them that they knew it by heart, all nine of them. The three then sat back under the park bench and looked up and enjoyed the view of the stars.'

The story ended. Noble wasn't sure what the story meant. He knew that there were lots of hints in the story but he would need time to figure it out. Although he never read the story until just then, there was something familiar with it that he couldn't grasp on just yet. But he had no time to analyze the story.

He took a deep breath and then looked at Kat.

"I have to help Blay," Noble said. "There's a chance I'll get caught. I think you should leave now so you won't be mixed up in this."

He walked up to Kat and gave her a hug. After a moment, Noble let go and started to walk away. But Kat grabbed his hand.

"You'll get caught in less than 24 hours," Kat said as she looked very concerned. "They'll find you."

"Maybe, but I have to try," Noble said.

"If you really want to do this, you're going to need my help," Kat said.

"No, I don't want you involve in this," Noble said.

"I'm already involved ever since I fell for you," Kat said. "I need you to go pack and I'll go get us a ride."

Noble looked confused while Kat was walking toward the front door.

"Our cars are in the garage," Noble said.

Kat turned around and said, "If we use our own cars, they'll find us for sure. I'm going to borrow the neighbor's car. I'll be right back."

Kat then left the house. Noble looked around and then started to pack.

Chapter 12

Nan and Remy lived across from Noble and Kat. They've been together for some time. They were having a nice conversation when their house announced to them that Kat was in front of their door. Nan went and opened the front door.

"Kat, it's good to see you. Please come in," Nan said.

"Thank you but maybe another time," Kat said. "Noble and I were supposed to meet up with Blay and his date for drinks, but our car has a malfunction. Can we borrow yours for the night?"

"Of course, but you must come in and have coffee with us first. We're celebrating," Nan said.

Kat hesitated for a split second and then smiled and said, "Sure."

She went inside and the door closed automatically. Kat didn't want to go in knowing she was running out of time, but she didn't want to resist the invitation too much with the chance her neighbors might get suspicious.

As soon as Kat was inside, Nan was already walking into the kitchen.

"Kat, how are you?" Remy asked as he went to Kat and gave her a hug.

"Great, Remy," Kat answered. "How are you?"

"Wonderful!" Remy said. "Did Nan tell you the good news yet?"

"No, not yet," Kat said.

Nan came out of the kitchen and handed Kat a cup of coffee.

"Here, try this," Nan said.

Kat took a sip from the cup and said, "Mmm...it's good coffee."

"So guess what?" Nan asked with excitement in her voice.

Kat smiled happily and shrugged her shoulders.

"I'm pregnant again!" Nan shouted joyously.

Kat put down her cup on the table and went up to Nan and gave her a big hug.

"That's so awesome!" Kat said.

"Yeah, we're very happy," Nan said. "Remy is especially thrilled, but he's also very worried."

"It'll be fine," Kat said. "You just have to be careful and take it easy."

"Our doctor said our chances are good this time," Nan said.

"But the doctor said the same thing the last time before the miscarriage," Remy said. "We have to be extra careful this time."

"I've already told my employer that I'm taking off for this," Nan said. "I'm staying home until our baby is delivered."

Kat kept the appearance of excitement for them. She didn't want to give them any indication that their plan would probably fail given what she just found out.

"I read the statistics that for pregnancy rate between an AIB and a human is just as good as between two humans, although both are still low," Nan said.

"You would think with all the advancements with our medical technology, we would be able to solve this problem," Remy said.

"Well, don't pay attention to the statistics," Kat said to Nan. "Just concentrate on yourself."

"I would've used champagne to celebrate tonight but with the pregnancy and all…," Nan explained.

"Perfectly fine," Kat said as she picked up her cup and took another sip and then placed it on the table.

"Well, I better go and let you get some rest," Kat said as she walked toward Nan and gave her a hug.

"Thanks Kat," Nan said. "Oh, I almost forgot. Let me give you the code to our car."

Nan tapped her HIDD and a holographic image appeared. She touched a few options on the menu and then pressed 'Send'.

"There, have fun tonight," Nan said. "I didn't even know Blay was dating someone."

"Thanks Nan," Kat said. "I think he met her just recently. I'll know soon enough and give you the juicy details."

"That'll be great," Nan said.

Kat hugged Nan one last time and said, "Goodnight."

"Night," Nan said.

The two started to walk to the front door as Remy said his goodnight to Kat. Kat left the house and headed straight to their car and got in. She immediately put the car in the manual mode and started to drive back to her house.

Chapter 13

Noble was in the bedroom when he saw Kat walking in.

"I got the car," she said. "Did you finish packing?"

"Yes," Noble said as he held up the duffle bag to show Kat.

"You have to change into something more mobile," Kat said as she saw Noble was still in his suit. "And no body suits. Even those are traceable."

As Noble was taking off his clothes, he was surprised that Kat was talking like she's done this before. He didn't want to discuss it with her at that point because they were in a rush to leave.

Kat headed straight to the closet and took out a duffle bag and placed it on the bed. She then immediately took her dress off and revealed a sexy black laced bra with matching thong. Noble realized then that she wasn't lying about the sexy lingerie. Kat then proceeded to take off her bra and thong, showing her perfect naked body. Noble would've been aroused if he wasn't so nervous. Kat then opened her duffle bag and took out an athletic bra and panties. She put them on quickly. She then took out a dark athletic shirt and pants and put them on as well. They were tightly fitted on her body. Next, she put her hair into a pony tail and tied it together with a hair band. After that, she went into her duffle bag once more and took out a cap and another HIDD. She put those on. The athletic shirt had a docking station for the HIDD by the left upper chest area.

"You ready?" Kat asked.

"Yeah," Noble said as he was now in a similar athletic shirt and pants as Kat.

"One last thing," Kat said. "I need you to transfer your files from your HIDD to this HIDD of mine."

"Why?" Noble asked.

"Because they can trace your HIDD," Kat explained as she was pointing to the HIDD on her chest. "They'll have a much harder time tracking this HIDD, which is a ghost HIDD."

"What are you doing with a ghost HIDD?" Noble asked.

"I'll explain later when we're on the road," Kat said. "But for now, please transfer your files. And after you do that, delete everything in your HIDD."

Kat's tone was very authoritative. Noble didn't want to waste more time asking her more questions, so he did as she said. He tapped open his HIDD and transferred all his files into Kat's ghost HIDD. Kat tapped open her ghost HIDD and verified that all the files were transferred, especially the one from Blay.

"Got it," Kat confirmed.

Noble then went and proceeded to delete all the files from his HIDD. A moment later, he got a message from his HIDD confirming all of his files were deleted.

"Good, now give me your HIDD," Kat said.

Noble handed his HIDD to Kat. Kat then went and grabbed her HIDD that she used every day. She placed both HIDDs on the dresser. She grabbed one of her high heeled shoes that she wore earlier and she used it to smash the two HIDDs with the heel of the shoe. After a few good smacks, the two HIDDs were smashed into pieces. Noble was surprised and impressed with the force Kat used in smacking the HIDDS.

"Okay, let's go," Kat said as she put on new athletic shoes. She grabbed her duffle bag and looked at Noble.

Noble grabbed his duffle bag and the two left the bedroom and headed for the front door. But before they left, Kat instructed the house to do one last thing.

"Total lockdown!" Kat said loudly.

The house responded and said, "Total lockdown confirmed."

The two then walked out of the house. As soon as they left, the door closed automatically and metal blinds began to slide down on the outside of the house to cover all the windows and doors. No one could break in.

"Let's hope that will slow them down a bit," Kat said.

The two then got into their neighbor's car with Kat in the driver's seat. A moment later, the car drove off.

Chapter 14

Creyson was sitting on the sofa looking around the room when he started to reflect how fortunate his life had been. He was born an AIB and remembered growing up under the Agency's care. He had only fond memories of his childhood. When he was eight, he was already excelling in academics. The Agency saw him as a potential teacher one day. But his focus turned to something else. He wanted to help the Agency in another way.

A hundred years ago, lawmakers around the world made a monumental achievement by eliminating nuclear weapons and vowed never to produce them ever again. Forty years after that, they did something even more radical. They decided to ban all military weapons, all chemical weapons and even all firearms. In the United States, that meant repealing the Second Amendment, which was a gigantic shift in the political world of the country. But when the rest of the world did just that, the U.S. had no other choice but to comply. Society was entering into a less deadly world. The most deadly weapons that were still legal were knives, swords and bows and arrows.

To police a world with little or no weapons, agents had to be retrained. Hand-to-hand combat became the choice of confrontation against combatants and law breakers. Close quarter combat (CQC) experts were sought after for the police force in the Agency. The practice of martial arts became the foundation of the combat techniques in the police world. Many veteran officers retired or left because of the change, but many signed up because of it including Creyson.

When Creyson turned 18, he applied for a police agent position with the Agency. He had to take an academic test, which he passed with flying colors. There was a physical test that he was prepared for. Creyson had started training with martial arts when he was eight and he loved it. He wasn't aware then that practicing martial arts was a good way to learn discipline nor was he aware he was getting great exercise. All he remembered was that he enjoyed it immensely.

Once Creyson graduated from the academy, his ambition drove him to work hard and solve cases. His instincts and analytical skills served him well. He loved catching criminals who plot against the Agency. After a couple of years in the field, he was quickly recognized as one of the top agents in the Agency. He was promoted to lead a team in his sector. But management was looking to place him to be lead instructor in their academy or promote him to upper management. But that would mean they would have to take him off the field. He turned down their offers because he loved being in the field. He claimed that's where the actions were.

Creyson had brief relationships, but not one of the women he dated could keep him committed in the relationship. He stopped dating and instead, preferred contacting women to come over for sex. He could get his sexual needs satisfied and not be in a relationship. All this were going through his head while he was waiting.

Agent One came up to Creyson.

"Sir, we've decrypted Blay's message," Agent One said.
Creyson got a message in his HIDD and he opened it. Agent One sent Blay's message to him. Creyson was reading the message thoroughly.

"So he sent it to his friend, Noble," Creyson said. "That means we still have time. The Purists doesn't have the file yet."

"No sir, he did not send it to them," Agent One said.

"Well, let's go and pay a visit to his friend, Noble," Creyson said as he got up from the sofa and leaving the house. Agent One followed right behind him.

Chapter 15

After being on the road for some time, Noble had an urge to ask Kat some questions but he kept looking back to check and see if they were being followed.

"Don't worry, we're not being followed…not yet anyway," Kat said.

"How do you know so much about evading the law?" Noble asked.

"With my line of work, I need a contingency plan just in case," Kat said.

"You're a makeup artist. How unlawful does that get?" Noble asked.

"Oh, I don't do anything illegal," Kat said. "But some of the clients that I get…well let's just say I don't want to know because I never ask them."

"Then why do you think you need a contingency plan to evade the law if you're not doing anything illegal?" Noble asked.

"Hang on," Kat said as she interrupted Noble.

Kat tapped her HIDD and said, "Slade, it's Kat. I need you."

A moment later she got a reply.

"Kat, how's my favorite artist?" Slade asked as his voice came through the car's speakers.

"Listen Slade, I need an exit package for two and I need it now," Kat said.

"For who?" Slade asked.

"Me and Noble," Kat answered.

"What's happened?" Slade asked.

"I'll explain it to you when I get there," Kat said.

There was a pause in the conversation.

"The late notice is going to cost you...say 30 million credits," Slade said.

"We both know that's too much," Kat said. "I'll give you 15 million."

"I can't do it for 15. I'll lose money," Slade said. "Make it 25 million."

"I'll do 18 million if you throw in a car for us," Kat said.

"I don't think you're in a position to negotiate with me," Slade said. "Because whatever you're running from seems serious. Desperate times come with a hefty price tag."

"That's fine by me," Kat said. "But I can't guarantee you that if I do get caught that they won't make me talk about your business and the clients that you have."

"Are you blackmailing me, girl?" Slade asked.

"No, I'm just giving you a logical conclusion of what would probably happen if you don't help us," Kat explained.

There was a pause for a moment.

"Fine, 18 million credits then," Slade said.

"Great, I need a pick up," Kat said. "I'll be at the usually spot."

"I'll send the car over now," Slade said. "It should be there in 30 minutes."

"Thanks Slade. You won't regret this," Kat said.

"I'm regretting it already," Slade said and then the line got disconnected.

"Who is this guy, Slade?" Noble asked with concern.

"Slade is a person I work with," Kat answered.

"What do you do for him?" Noble asked.

"Slade brings me appointments for people who need me to apply makeup for them," Kat said. "Some of them don't appear to have high moral standards."

"You mean they're criminals?" Noble asked.

"I don't know since I don't ask them anything except for the makeup part," Kat said.

"What kind of makeup do you apply for them?" Noble asked.

"It's called contouring. It's an old art," Kat said. "I can actually apply the makeup on the person's face and change their appearance to the point that they look like someone else. I'm really good at it."

Noble was shocked. He needed a moment to process the information.

"So you help criminals change their appearance to evade the law?" Noble asked.

"I suspect many of them aren't criminals," Kat said. "Some of them look like they do it as a fantasy to be someone else, most do it to cheat on their partners and others do look like criminals but I never verify that."

"Why would you do that?" Noble asked.

"Because I'm an artist. It's what I do," Kat said. "Besides, I get paid very well for what I do."

"That's why you get paid in credits because it's much harder to trace," Noble said.

"Hence the ghost HIDD so I can access my ghost account," Kat said.

"And you don't think what you're doing is illegal?" Noble asked.

"Like you said earlier, I'm only doing makeup," Kat said. "If I don't know anything about my clients, then I have plausible deniability. I shouldn't be arrested nor prosecuted for doing just makeup for them."

Noble appeared to be unconvinced and Kat saw that.

"I have turned down clients from Slade when I found out they were fugitives," Kat said. "So I'm careful with the clients I take in."

"If you really feel that way, then why even have a contingency plan where you have a duffle bag ready to go in our closet?" Noble asked.

"Because the law could catch up to Slade at any time and I don't know if he would implicate me to save his own ass," Kat said. "Or it could be my clients' enemies that want to track me down thinking I might know where my clients went."

"That sounds dangerous," Noble said.

"Like I said, I love what I do and I'm good at it," Kat said. "The pay is great and I can take care of myself."

"Who are you?" Noble asked rhetorically.

"You're disappointed," Kat said.

"I don't know if I should be disappointed or impressed," Noble said. "It's like there's a whole different side of you."

"I'm still me," Kat said. "I don't tell you everything I do at work just like you don't tell me everything you do at work."

"That's because my work is mostly classified," Noble said.

"So are mine…in a way," Kat said.

Noble thought about that for a moment and then said, "Fair enough."

The car kept going until Kat began to see a parking lot.

"We're here," Kat said as she pulled into a parking lot. She could see another car on the lot. She thought it was most likely there waiting to pick them up. They stopped and got out of their car. They walked toward the other car parked in the lot and the doors opened automatically. Kat assumed Slade would've programmed the car to allow Kat in. Kat got into the car and Noble soon followed. The car started to move by itself and then it drove out of the parking lot.

"Where are we going? Noble asked.

"Vice City," Kat said.

Chapter 16

An air pod was descending on the front lawn of Noble's house. It was big and could carry twenty people. It landed smoothly with little noise. Creyson and three of his agents got out of the air pod and walked toward the front door. Creyson noticed the metal blinds covering the windows and doors. He realized that Noble was probably gone but he still had to go in and look for clues of where Noble went. His agents were able to decrypt who the message was sent to but they were still working on opening the message so that they could read the contents of the message.

"How long will it take to open the door?" Creyson asked.

"Five minutes, sir," Agent Two said.

Creyson nodded and started to walk around the house. He couldn't see any opening into the house and thought Noble knew they were coming. Noble probably got the heads up from the message, Creyson thought. He walked back toward the front door and saw Agent Two was still trying to open the blinds from the door.

"Almost there, sir," Agent Two said.

Creyson looked around the neighborhood to see if anything looked out of place and nothing did. He even thought that the neighborhood was really nice, very suburban. He would even live here if he was looking for a place.

Then Creyson heard the sound of the metal blinds moving up from the door and windows. The door then opened automatically. Creyson could hear the house said, "Alarm overridden."

Creyson went into the house immediately and his three agents followed right behind him. He walked to the center of the house and started to pan around. His three agents walked around to different areas of the house. A moment later, Creyson could hear Agent One called for him.

"Sir, there's something here in the bedroom you should see," Agent One said.

Creyson proceeded into the bedroom. He saw Agent One pointing to the pieces of the HIDDs that were smashed. Creyson realized then that not only did Noble knew they were coming, but Noble also ditched his HIDD and possibly all other electronics he had on him, making it much more difficult to track him down. But Creyson knew he had to track down Noble before Noble could retrieve the file and use it against the Agency. He turned to the bedroom door and walked out. Agent One followed him out.

Creyson was walking the hallway when Agent Two and Three met up with him.

"We didn't find anything unusual, sir," Agent Three said

Creyson paused a moment to think. Then he proceeded to walk toward the garage with his three agents following him. When the door to the garage opened automatically, Creyson immediately noticed there were two vehicles still in the garage. He quickly turned around and pointed to Agent Two and Three.

"You two, check the house again and make sure they're still not here hiding," Creyson said. "And make sure there are no hidden rooms."

The two agents nodded and left to check the house again.

Creyson then looked at Agent One and said, "Someone else was living with him. Find out who it is now."

"Yes sir," Agent One said and walked away from Creyson.

Creyson then turned around and looked at the vehicles again. He was thinking that Noble left in a way that the Agency can't track him. Creyson was a little impressed but surprised that a theoretical physicist would know how to evade the law. Perhaps the message Noble got instructed him, Creyson thought but he won't know until he got more information. He then turned and walked back to the bedroom.

In the bedroom, Creyson looked down at the debris and then noticed something a few feet away from the area, a high heeled shoe. He walked toward it and bent down to retrieve the shoe. It was a nice and fancy shoe, he thought. He then stood up and walked toward the closet. He opened the closet door and saw lots of clothes, for a man and a woman. Creyson was wondering who the woman was. The initial report of this address didn't mention anything about anyone living with Noble.

Later on, Agents Two and Three reported to Creyson that there were no hidden rooms nor anyone else in the house. Soon after that, Agent One approached Creyson.

"Sir, Noble is living with a female. Her name is Kat," Agent One said. "We don't have any information on her except that she's an AIB."

The word AIB tweeted Creyson's interest particularly.

Agent One continued, "Sir, it's highly unusual that we have very little information on someone. It's like…she's…a…"

"A ghost," Creyson said as he helped Agent One finished the sentence.

"Yes sir," Agent One said.

Creyson appeared upset.

"Shit! She's helping him," Creyson said irritatingly and walked out of the house. The three agents followed him.

Creyson was in the front yard looking around and concluded the two wouldn't have left on foot.

"Was any car or air service contacted for this area?" Creyson asked Agent One. "Check the illegitimate services that are in our files also."

Agent One tapped his HIDD and started to touch the holographic menus.

"No sir," Agent One said. "No service was called."

"Did Noble contact any of his friends or associates besides Kat?" Creyson asked.

Agent One checked for a moment and then said, "No sir."

Creyson was pissed that he didn't have any information on Kat or any of her associates. He seemed a bit frustrated. He then took a few steps and looked around the neighborhood. Creyson kept thinking it was such a nice neighborhood. Then he thought that with nice neighborhood, came nice neighbors.

"Check the neighbors. Starting with this one, that one and that one," Creyson said as he was pointing to the three houses around.

The three agents immediately started to jog to the three houses. Shortly after they left, Agent Two ran back to Creyson.

"Sir, the neighbors in that house said Kat came to them a few hours ago and borrowed their car," Agent Two said.

"Where's the car now?" Creyson asked.

"I was able to track it to a parking lot about 70 miles south from here," Agent Two said.

"Let's go!" Creyson said firmly.

The four rushed back into the air pod. A brief moment later, it quietly lifted off and ascended high in the air. The air pod then quickly accelerated and flew away.

Chapter 17

The city had a formal name decades ago, but residents and visitors alike all called it Vice City. No one knew how it came to be, except for the reputation the city exhumed. Any illegal activities one was able to think of could be found in Vice City as if the city was an unofficial hub for the alleged criminals to meet and conduct their businesses. It was a place where they were able to express their entrepreneurial prowess. Many of them felt what they were doing were not illegal…unless they got caught.

This was how Slade operated ever since he started his enterprise ten years ago when he was just eighteen years old. He had a gift not in academics, but at looking at an opportunity no one else saw or wanted to see and exploits it. The niche he found ten years ago was a service to provide his clients a different identity if they were willing to pay a handsome price for it. The idea was to find people willing to give up their identity to a buyer who wants it. The buyer would pay the seller a large fee to take their identity for a period of time. The fee range was depended on the length of time the buyer would need the new identity.

The buyer not only would be able to use the seller's identity, but he or she could also access all their accounts and especially the most important one, their HIDD account. So the buyer could control the new identity more fully. To add to the transformation, Slade would find the buyer a seller that most resembled the buyer physically. The program algorithm in his computers would conduct all the photo comparisons. After the potential seller had been selected by the computer, then the seller would be contacted. The sellers would already have a set price based on the length of the request and the amount of time the notice was given to the seller. Usually the shorter the notice, the higher the price would be. This included the time frame; the longer the identity was being requested, the higher the price the buyer had to pay.

To complete the transformation, Slade would have the buyer come in to meet Kat, his favorite and best artist. From there, Kat would use her artistic skills to transform the buyer to look like the seller using contouring techniques with her makeup. The applied makeup can be good for 24 to 48 hours without any touchup as long as the buyer didn't wash the face or perspire too much. After that was done, Slade would provide the buyer a duplicate HIDD from the seller to use. The transformation or the exit package would be completed at that point. He had a nice loft in a big warehouse building in Vice City to conduct his business. The loft had separate studios for the makeup artists to work their craft on the clients.

To avoid being caught for all parties, the money would change hands through ghost currency. The buyer would set up a ghost account with none of his or her personal information in it through a ghost currency service. The buyer would just get an account number and a PIN password. The buyer would then exchange his or her regular currency for ghost credits through a third party company. That company would then deposit the ghost currency into the buyer's ghost account. The buyer could then pay the seller the fee using ghost credits.

Slade considered himself the middleman in the transaction. His service was to find sellers and buyers. For his service, he would charge a premium fee for it. Not surprisingly, there were always buyers needing this kind of service. He didn't' believe it was illegal although the law labeled it as illegal. Slade considered it more like a buyer fulfilling a fantasy to be someone else even though he didn't truly believe in that explanation. But that would be his defense if he ever got caught with the law. He knew that some of the clients he had gotten were shady characters who wanted to hide from the law but he was smart enough to never ask them the important question of why.

The seller would benefit from using the ghost account. In case the buyer does get caught and the law reached the seller, the seller could always claim identity theft and say he or she knew nothing about any of it. The seller would not know the buyer and vice versa. Plus, ghost accounts were virtually untraceable. Most criminals preferred dealing in ghost currency using their ghost accounts.

So Slade was surprised when Kat contacted him needing exit packages for two people. He already had a seller for Kat because that's what Kat requested before coming onboard. Kat was smart enough to get an escape plan before starting work. All Slade had to do was to find a seller for Noble. Since Slade never met Noble or knew what Noble looked like, he would have to wait until they arrived to match a seller for Noble. But as soon as Slade finished his thoughts, Kat and Noble walked in.

Chapter 18

"Do you have the exit packages ready?" Kat asked Slade.

"Well, hello to you too," Slade said. "I have yours ready but I need to find your boyfriend here a seller. I didn't know what he looked like."

Kat took Noble's hand and guided him to a spot in front of Slade and said, "Don't move."

Noble was looking at Slade and wasn't moving. He thought that Slade was young and looked like he could be a computer guy. If Slade had walked next to him on the street, Noble wouldn't have thought he was a criminal.

"Got it?" Kat asked Slade.

"Yeah, I got it," Slade said as he uploaded Noble's 3D image into his computer.

"Good, I'll be in my studio getting ready," Kat said. "Let me know when you have Noble's exit package ready."

"Wait, what the hell did you get yourself into?" Slade asked. "We've always been very careful."

"I can't tell you," Kat said. "Believe me, you don't want to know. You and I don't ask the clients why they need the service, remember?"

"Yeah, but if you leave, I'll be losing my best makeup artist," Slade said.

"You'll still have plenty of makeup artists to choose from," Kat said. "Granted, none of them are better than me."

"We'll have to renegotiate on the price," Slade insisted.

"Bullshit! I've done plenty of jobs and last minute favors for you and you're making plenty on this deal," Kat said.

"But I'll be losing potential income once you leave," Slade said.

"When I get back, I'll help you double your business," Kat said.

"We both know you won't be coming back anytime soon," Slade said.

Kat sighed.

At that moment, Slade noticed his computer found a match to a seller for Noble.

"Looks like your boyfriend's new name is Tyler," Slade said.

"Great! Send the file to my studio," Kat said and then she turned around and walked toward the studio across the room. Noble followed right behind her.

As soon as they went into Kat's studio, Kat closed the door for privacy. She then pointed to the studio chair in the center of the room.

"Sit down," Kat instructed Noble.

Noble went and sat on the chair. Kat then walked over to the makeup table next to the chair. There was a button on top of the table. Kat pushed the button. A holographic image of a man appeared. The man looked similar to Noble.

"I have to make you look like him," Kat said. "So be patient. It'll take some tlme."

"This is what you do?" Noble asked. "You can make me look like him?"

"You'll know when I'm done," Kat said.

Kat went to the drawer of the makeup table and took some things out and placed them on the table. She began with using a moist cloth to clean Noble's face. Once his face was dried, Kat applied a primer so the makeup would hold up longer after the makeup application. After that, she applied the foundation which was the most important part. The foundation had to match the new person's skin color and tone. She mapped the face with the foundation and then she layered the foundation so it looked more natural. She then used different shades of foundations to make Noble look more like the guy in the image. After that, she concentrated on his eyes and worked on them for some time. She had to use some mascara and eyeliner on him.

When Kat was done, she pushed another button on the makeup table. This time it was Noble with his makeup on. His face was next to the seller's face.

"Hello Tyler," Kat said.

Noble couldn't believe it. His face was strikingly similar to this Tyler person.

"You are amazing!" Noble said impressively.

"I know," Kat said.

"I thought you did makeup, but I didn't think it was something like this," Noble said.

"Just don't rub or wash your face for now," Kat said. "I put a lot of hard work into it."

Noble nodded.

"Now I need the chair so I can do myself," Kat said.

Noble got off the chair and then Kat sat down and started to put makeup on herself.

"This shouldn't take long," Kat said. "I've done Sabrina's face before for practice."

"That's your new name?" Noble asked.

"You like it?" Kat asked.

"Yes," Noble answered.

Noble was looking at Kat and thought how impressed he was with her. She's been handling all this without fear. The Agency is after them and she knew how to evade them. She appeared so confident like everything was going to be fine.

"Can you open up Blay's story?" Noble asked. "I want to try to decipher it."

Kat tapped her HIDD and after a brief moment, the holographic image of the story appeared. She handed the HIDD to Noble. He was reading it again.

Chapter 19

"It's a map of some sort, isn't it?" Kat asked as she was putting the final touches of the makeup on her face, not looking at Noble.

"Yes, it's instructions to tell us where it is," Noble said as he was reading it again. "Blay was confident that I would be able to solve it. He wouldn't make it so difficult that it would take me days or even weeks to solve it."

"What is the story trying to say?" Kat said.

"I've never read this story but somehow it's familiar to me," Noble said.

"What does your gut feeling tell you?" Kat asked.

"My gut feeling is telling me that the numbers in the story are coordinates," Noble answered.

"You mean like latitude and longitude?" Kat asked.

"Precisely," Noble said. "See, the first week the squirrel collected should be the latitude, 6.0883. The period comes after the six because the squirrel decided to take a break for a period of time."

"So the second week is longitude and that should be 11.2693," Kat said.

"No, it should be -11.2693 because the squirrel is taking the nuts, making the number negative," Noble said.

Noble went to the HIDD and picked a menu for Maps. He plugged those numbers in and the coordinates showed the location was somewhere in the North Atlantic Ocean, a little to the west of Africa. Noble thought him and Blay never went to that part of the world before.

"It's somewhere in the ocean?" Kat asked.

"It wouldn't be this easy in case the Agency intercepted the message," Noble said. "Blay would've left me a key to open the message."

As he read the story over and over again, something became very familiar to him. He was surprised he didn't see it before. The names were familiar to him. Then he realized the squirrel, Max, had the key. He multiplied a number with the coordinates and plugged in the new coordinates into the map. A moment later, he was happy with joy. He found the location.

"I know where it is. We have to go to Princeton," Noble said.

"I'm finished. We can go," Kat said.

Noble felt a bit strange seeing Kat looking like someone else. She's still just as beautiful, he thought. The two walked out of the studio and back to Slade.

"Hey, strangers," Slade said. "Don't you two turned out nice?"

"We have to go," Kat said to Slade. "Just make sure you delete everything about us."

"You know I always do," Slade said as he handed the new HIDDs to Kat and Noble.

"Thanks Slade," Kat said.

"The price you paid is good for a month," Slade said. "After that, I can't guarantee if the HIDDs or the identities would be compromised or not."

"Hopefully we won't need it for that long," Kat said.

"Hopefully not, for all our sakes because whoever you're running from sounds serious," Slade said. "Should I be prepared to run too before they get here?"

Kat sighed and thought Slade deserved to know. They had a good working relationship.

"The Agency is coming for us," Kat said. "We have to find Hunter so he can help us. He's the leader for the Purists."

"Shit!" Slade shouted. "You got the Agency coming after you two?"

"We just have to delay them until we can find Hunter," Kat said.

"Girl, you know the Purists hate you and all other AIBs in the world," Slade said. "What makes you think Hunter will help you?"

"Because we have something that he wants," Kat said. "Do you know where I can find Hunter?"

Slade sighed and then said, "I don't know where exactly, but he's somewhere in Philadelphia."

"How can we get in touch with him?" Kat asked.

"There's a club called Sinner's Maze," Slade said. "Ask for Jumma, the manager. She can help you with that."

"Thanks Slade," Kat said as she went and gave Slade a hug.

"Looks like I'll be closing my shop earlier than expected," Slade said.

"Just think, you made enough to retire already," Kat said.

"I am a man with expensive taste," Slade said. "I need more money to sustain my lifestyle."

Kat smiled and said, "Goodbye Slade. I really hope we meet again."

Kat walked toward the front door. Before Noble followed Kat, he walked over to Slade, shook Slade's hand and said, "Thank you, Slade."

"Take good care of her," Slade said.

"I will," Noble said and then he left with Kat.

Chapter 20

"The what constant?" Kat asked.

Kat and Noble were now in a vehicle that was driving them to Princeton.

"It's the Planck constant," Noble said. "It's a physical constant that is the quantum of action. It was created by a great mathematician by the name of Max Planck who the constant was named after."

"How did you know Max the squirrel is about Max Planck?" Kat asked.

"I didn't until I found out who Max's friends are," Noble said.

"Who are they?" Kat asked.

"Bert and Al are not two individuals, they're one," Noble said. "And it's Al and Bert or Albert...as in Einstein."

"How did you know it was Einstein?" Kat asked.

"Because Al and Bert didn't believe the creator did things by chance," Noble said. "And neither did Einstein."

"How are Einstein and Max Planck related?" Kat asked.

"It turns out that the two were good friends," Noble said. "Einstein even used the Planck constant on some of his equations."

"But how did you come up with that number?" Kat asked.

"In the story, Max the squirrel is always stressing on the word constant or constantly and the number nine," Noble said. "The first nine digits of the Plank constant are 6.62607004. I just multiplied the coordinates with that number."

"So the Planck constant is like pi, a constant number?" Kat asked.

"Yes. Pi is more commonly known. But the Planck constant is less known. If one is not dealing with advanced math or physics, one would never need it," Noble said. "The actual Planck constant is 6.62607004×10 to the -34, but we're just using the first nine digits. And Blay knew that I knew this because I told him about Max Planck."

"And you think that's right?" Kat asked.

"I think it's our best shot," Noble said. "The coordinates show a park in Princeton. And to improve our odds, the park is close to where Albert Einstein used to live. It's got to be there because I took Blay there one time to tour the area."

"Blay knew you knew where it was," Kat said.

Noble nodded.

After another thirty minutes of driving, the vehicle eventually stopped in front of the park. Noble and Kat got out of the vehicle and they ran into the park. Noble was scanning around.

"It's a big park," Kat said. "Where do we begin?"

Noble was looking around and thinking where Blay could've hid the file. Then he remembered in the story that Max the squirrel liked hanging under a park bench. Noble was looking around the park for park benches. He saw three that were visible to him.

"Try the park benches," Noble said. "Look underneath because the squirrel in the story liked to look up from under the bench."

"I'll take that one," Kat said as she pointed to one of the benches. She ran over to the bench and looked around for anything. She looked underneath and found nothing.

She looked over to Noble as he was looking around the bench he selected and found nothing either. Then he looked up and at Kat and pointed to the bench on the other side of the park and Kat nodded. Noble ran over to the third bench and started to look. There was nothing on the bench. Noble got down to the ground and looked underneath the bench. A quick glance showed nothing, but then Noble slowed down and looked again and he noticed a piece of duct tape stuck underneath the bench. There was something that bulged out of the tape. Noble took the piece of the duct tape off and got the object the duct tape was holding.

"I found something!" Noble shouted.

Kat was running toward him.

Noble was looking at a dice and then he remembered Blay's story '...play dice with the park.'

"You found it," Kat said.

Noble looked closer at the dice and noticed there was a tiny line cut across the dice. He tried to pull the sides open but couldn't. Then he tried to twist it open like a bottle and it began to twist open. When the dice opened, it had a secret compartment. The file chip was lying inside.

"I found it," Noble said.

Chapter 21

The air pod descended onto the parking lot. It made little noise when it landed. The door opened and Creyson walked out along with his three agents. Creyson was looking around the parking lot while the three agents approached the car. Why would the vehicle stopped at a parking lot out of nowhere, he wondered. The obvious answer Creyson thought was that they were meeting someone else or someone else was here to pick them up. It was a smart move to avoid being tracked, he thought.

Agent One returned back to Creyson.

"Sir, the vehicle does belong to Noble's neighbor," Agent One reported. "It hasn't been active for hours so they could be anywhere by now. There were no recent car service activities in the area either."

Creyson looked around the area and thought for a moment.

"She's good," Creyson said. "Now I really like to meet her."

He then walked around the parking lot and kept looking all over the area. It helped his thinking process. Someone must've came and picked them up. That was the most logical explanation, Creyson thought.

Creyson was impressed with how Kat was able to stay under the radar. Her skills of evading the law didn't come overnight, he thought. There's only one place close to the area where they would've gone to evade the law, and it wasn't too far from here. It was then that he had a pretty good idea where they went.

"We're going to Vice City," Creyson said.

He then turned around and headed toward the air pod. The rest of his agents followed. As soon as they went into the air pod, it took off quietly and quickly accelerated into the sky.

In less than half an hour, the air pod arrived at Vice City. Creyson knew the area well. He made his name in this city of criminals. He caught smugglers, money launderers, drug dealers and extortionists. But the one group he hated the most and got the most satisfaction of catching is the Purists. Creyson considered them as anti-government terrorists. These people would murder AIBs for their cause. Creyson didn't believe violence was the answer, no matter how strongly one believed in something.

The Purists hated AIBs since the beginning. They believed the AIBs had no place in society and should all die or serve the humans. They don't believe the AIBs should have gotten their independence. Creyson thought the Purists had a limited view of the world. But the government was not able to classify the Purists as a terrorist organization because only a handful of them were caught as murderers. But they don't hide their hatred against the AIBs. The Purists openly protested against the AIBs in their speeches and in their writings. Creyson concluded it was the price being paid for free speech.

All four of them got out of the air pod with Creyson leading the way. He looked around the area and knew everyone in the area was looking at them. Everyone in the city hated having the law around the streets. They were not able to conduct their businesses and be themselves when the law was around. Creyson looked at one of the establishments and knew it was a place to launder money. He busted the owner before who had to spend a year in federal penitentiary. He decided to walk to the establishment. His three agents waited outside of the store.

"Oh shit! Creyson!" Flak, the owner of the store, said nervously when Creyson walked into the store.

"I need information, Flak," Creyson said.

"Hey, I'm a legitimate business man now," Flak said. "I can't help you."

"Really? You mean if my agents start going through all your account transactions, they're not going to find anything unusual?" Creyson asked.

Flak sighed and asked, "Why are you hassling me?"

"Why wouldn't I hassle you?" Creyson asked rhetorically.

"I'm small time…I'm just trying to make a living," Flak said. "I've already spent a year in jail. Can't you give me a break?"

"Relax, I'm not here for you…if you give me the information that I need," Creyson said. "I know you know everything that's going on in this city."

Flak sighed and asked, "What do you want to know?"

"I need to find a girl named Kat," Creyson said. "She's an AIB and is good at keeping herself hidden."

"I don't know anyone like that but I can ask around," Flak said. "But you have to give me some time."

Creyson was disappointed with that answer but thought of another question to ask.

"Who's the best in the business of helping people to evade the law around here?" Creyson asked.

Flak looked hesitant.

"Well?" Creyson asked insistently.

"If I tell you, then he'll know it was me who did it," Flak said.

"If you don't tell me, then I'll haul you in instead," Creyson said. "You decide, but do it fast because my patience is running out."

Flak grumbled and hesitantly said, "Slade is the best in the city. He offers the best exit packages."

"And where can I find this Slade?" Creyson asked.

"He conducts his business in that warehouse building over there," Flak said as he was pointing to the building through the window.

Creyson turned and looked at the building and said, "Thanks, that's all I needed."

Creyson was about to leave when Flak said, "Hey, we didn't' have this conversation."

Creyson rolled his eyes and turned back to Flak and said, "A bunch of people on the street saw me walking in here so I'm sure they knew we had a conversation."

Creyson walked out of the store and his three agents were waiting for him just outside of the store.

"Let's visit the warehouse," Creyson said while looking at the warehouse.

Back in the store, Flak looked upset and then he tapped his HIDD and dialed for Slade.

"Yeah?" Slade asked as his holographic image appeared.

"Sorry Slade, I had no choice," Flak said. "The Agency is coming for you."

Chapter 22

Slade already knew the Agency was coming to look for him before Flak called but he didn't really expect them to come so early. At least Flak had the decency of calling and gave him a heads up even though Flak was the one who gave him up, Slade thought.

Slade had to move quickly. He took out his HIDD from his chest and placed it in a docking station next to his computers. He then logged into his computer and started typing. The holographic screen popped up and asked, 'Move all files?' Slade used his finger and touched the 'Yes' button. The computers then started downloading all the stored files to the HIDD.

It took about two minutes but the holographic screen eventually showed 'Files transfer completed.' Slade then took his HIDD out of the docking station and attached it back on his chest. He then started to type on the keyboard. They were instructions to erase all the files in all the computers. He didn't want to leave any evidence that could incriminate him. The holographic screen showed, 'Delete all files?' Again, Slade touched the 'Yes' button. The computers began to erase all the files.

As soon as Slade pushed the 'Yes' button to delete all his files, he looked up and saw four men running up the stairs toward his floor through his security cameras. Slade had seen enough agents from the Agency to recognize that those men were probably the men that were with Flak earlier. Slade then started running to the back door. He hated to leave all his work behind but he had no choice. He had a good run for the last ten years of not getting caught, but he realized the law would catch up to him one day. So he ran down to the lobby and out of the warehouse. He didn't look back because there was no reason to do so.

Creyson and his agents arrived at the front door of Slade's flat. He knocked on the door and announced that it was the Agency but on one answered. Creyson had a feeling that Slade already knew they were coming.

"Knock it down!" Creyson shouted.

Agent One began kicking the door open. After a few tries, the front door broke and it opened for them. The four rushed in. Creyson didn't' see anyone in the flat but he quickly saw the computers and they were still erasing files but were almost done with the task.

"Stop the computers!" Creyson commanded.

Agent Two jumped right in on the chair by the computers and started typing on the keyboard. He was typing very quickly. It appeared he stopped the computers from erasing additional files.

The other two agents were walking around the whole flat to see if there was anyone still hiding. Creyson saw the computers and the makeup studios after he had a chance to go through the whole flat and thought that it was a nice business establishment. He was surprised he didn't know about Slade's operation. You just can't catch everyone, Creyson thought. Besides, identity alterations or thefts were considered less severe crimes. They were small fish. Creyson wanted to go after the big fish.

After a few minutes, Creyson walked toward Agent Two who was still typing by the computers.

"Sir, I was able to stop the deletion process but most of the files are gone already," Agent Two said. "It's going to take a few weeks to retrieve those files."

Creyson appeared upset.

"Are there any good news?" Creyson asked angrily.

Agent One walked toward Creyson and said, "Sir, our office was able to decrypt the message Blay sent to Noble."

"Show me," Creyson said.

Agent One tapped his HIDD and the message from Blay appeared in a holographic video. Creyson was listening to Blay's message tentatively. Then he read the story about the squirrels. He had to read it a few times to let it sink in. Then he began his routine of walking around the crime scene so he could think about the new information he just got.

Creyson concluded that Noble probably found the file already. He didn't believe Noble had given the file to Hunter yet because the news would've hit the public already. The Purists loved to show any dirt against the AIBs every chance they could get. Until now, what they had were minor and petty information. But the information Noble had was so major that it could ruin the future of the AIBs. The Purists would love to show it to the world immediately, if they had it.

Creyson looked around the area again to see if anything was out of place. Then he noticed a surveillance camera by the ceiling of the flat above the computer area. Slade didn't trust anyone, Creyson thought.

"Are the surveillance video erased?" Creyson asked Agent Two.

Agent Two was typing and then said, "Not all of them. The last 48 hours are still on file."

Creyson was relieved and thought they may be in luck.

"Show the video," Creyson said.

Agent Two typed some more and then a holographic video of the surveillance video appeared. It showed just Slade in the flat. "Fast forward," Creyson said.

A moment later, the video fast forwarded. There was nothing worth slowing down until the video showed Kat and Noble walking in.

"Stop," Creyson said. "Play normal speed."

The video showed Slade talking with Kat and Noble. The video showed the backs of Kat and Noble. It also showed Slade on his side talking.

"Zoom in on his face," Creyson said while pointing to Slade's head. "Can we read his lips?"

"No sir," Agent Two said.

Creyson sighed and said, "Continue with the video."

The video kept playing. It showed Kat and Noble walking into a studio room. The video kept playing until the two walked out and toward Slade. Their backs were toward the camera so Creyson couldn't get a good look at them. But this time, Slade's head was more toward the camera but a part of his lips was blocked by Kat's head.

"Zoom in on Slade's face," Creyson said. "Can we read his lips now?"

"His lips are partially blocked but…," Agent Two said as he was analyzing the lip movements of Slade. "…think Hunter will help you…he's somewhere in Philadelphia…Sinner's Maze…Jumma, the manager."

This was it, Creyson thought and decided his new strategy was to find this Jumma in Philadelphia. He was guessing that Noble and Kat were probably on their way to her. If he could get to Jumma first, then he could wait for Noble and Kat to arrive and then capture them. It was the best plan he could come up with at the moment.

"It's time to go to Philadelphia," Creyson said. "And I want to know everything about this Jumma person before we arrive there."

Creyson then walked quickly out of the flat. His three agents followed right behind him.

Chapter 23

Philadelphia was the birth place of The United States of America. It was where Thomas Jefferson, John Adams and Benjamin Franklin took major roles in contributing to the Declaration of Independence. In the end, it was Thomas Jefferson who penned the mighty document. It was in this city that Noble and Kat arrived, hoping to find Jumma. To their advantage, Slade already gave them the location of where to find her.

"We should be at the club soon," Kat said as the vehicle kept on driving by itself.

Noble nodded and looked out the car window.

"Are you okay?" Kat asked.

"Yeah," Noble said as he turned and looked back at Kat. "I still can't believe what's happening."

"We'll get through this," Kat said.

The driverless vehicle arrived at Sinner's Maze. But before they stopped, Kat ordered the vehicle to drive around the block so she could check if there were any officers or agents in the area. It was night time already so visibility was limited but Kat did the best she could. After not noticing anyone, she ordered the vehicle to park at the back of the club. Then they both got out of the vehicle and walked quickly into the club.

When they went in, they could see the place looked very sleek and modern. It was definitely a place to lounge and lay back. One would enjoy ordering a drink, then sit back and have a good time. Judging by the crowd, the place was very popular. It was definitely catered to the younger crowd.

Kat and Noble decided to walk toward the bar to talk to the bartender. The male bartender looked young and friendly.

"It's Jumma here?" Kat asked.

"Is everything okay with the service?" The bartender asked.

"The service is fine," Kat said. "We just like to talk to her."

"And who are you?" The bartender asked.

"We're friends of Blay," Kat said.

The bartender looked surprise and said, "Wait here." He then left the area.

Kat and Noble waited by the bar.

A moment later, a woman in her late 20's appeared with the bartender. She had short hair and looked very attractive. She also looked tough, like she could handle herself if things went south.

"I'm Jumma," she said. "You two are friends of Blay?"

"Yes," Noble said.

"Follow me," Jumma said and turned around and started to walk toward her office.

Noble and Kat both followed Jumma. They all went inside to her office. It was big and the lighting was dimmed. It had a lounge sofa but they all stood.

Jumma took out a device that was hidden in a wall shelf. It was small enough to be held in her hand. She walked up to Noble and started to wave the device all around his body.

"What are you doing?" Noble asked.

"Checking the amount of NIBs you have in your body to see if you're human or an AIB," Jumma said. "AIBs have a lot higher concentration of NIBs in their bodies than humans. We Purists already took out the NIBs in our bodies."

"You could've just asked," Noble said.

"I could, but this is the first time we've met. Try to understand that I am not going to just take your word for it," Jumma said.

Jumma was done waving the device around Noble's body. She looked at the device display and said, "You're human."

Jumma approached Kat as if she was about to wave the device around Kat's body, but Kat stuck her right arm and hand out to gesture Jumma to stop.

"I'm an AIB," Kat said to Jumma.

Jumma then backed off from Kat.

"You don't look like the picture Blay showed us," Jumma said to Noble.

"We had to disguise ourselves because the Agency is after us," Noble explained.

"Do you have the file?" Jumma asked.

"Yes, but I want to meet and talk to Hunter first," Noble said.

"Why don't you just hand me the file so the two of you don't have to be involved in this?" Jumma asked.

"No, Blay wanted me to hand the file over to Hunter personally," Noble said. "I want to meet him and talk to him before I give him the file."

"How do I know you really have the file?" Jumma asked.

Noble tapped his HIDD and selected the file. A holographic image appeared showing the core codes of COZ. Jumma was able to read them and was stunned.

"Mother of God," Jumma said.

A moment later, Noble turned off the hologram.

"Take us to Hunter," Noble said

Jumma nodded and said, "Alright, but your girlfriend has to stay behind. AIBs are not allowed in where we're going."

"She's coming with me," Noble said. "I trust her with my life."

Jumma hesitated for a moment.

"Look, if you want the file, then both of us have to go together," Noble said insistently. "We're not splitting apart."

Jumma thought for a moment and finally relented.

"Alright, she can come," Jumma said. "Follow me."

The three left the club and were waiting outside by the curb. A driverless vehicle pulled up in front of them. The doors opened automatically.

"Get in," Jumma said as she went into the vehicle.

Noble and Kat followed Jumma into the vehicle.

The ride took about fifteen minutes. No one talked the whole time. It was nighttime and there were people walking on the streets. The vehicle eventually pulled up to a building. It looked like a tall office building. The building looked new and modern. The vehicle stopped and its doors opened.

"We're here," Jumma said and got out of the vehicle.

Noble and Kat followed right behind her. The three walked inside the building and toward the elevator. The doors of the elevator opened automatically. The three went inside.

"Basement," Jumma said.

The elevator doors closed and the elevator headed down to the basement. When it reached the basement, the doors opened. There were four guards meeting them by the elevator already. Jumma walked out as if she didn't see them with Noble and Kat following behind her. The four guards were now walking behind them. A moment later, they all arrived at a door with two guards who were posted there. One of them opened the door for Jumma. They all walked into the room.

There was a man in his 50's standing in the room. He looked tall and in good shape. He was wearing a black suit.

The man looked at Noble and said, "Noble, my name is Hunter. I'm glad we finally meet."

Chapter 24

"Please, have a seat," Hunter said as he directed his new guests to some chairs.

Noble and Kat sat down while Jumma stood next to Hunter who sat down in his chair.

"Can I get you something to drink?" Hunter asked.

"Thank you but no," Noble replied.

"I'm sorry about your friend, Blay," Hunter said. "But I am grateful for what he did and for what you're doing now."

"The world needs to know," Noble said. "Blay believes you're the man to do that."

"Our organization has been around since the birth of the AIBs," Hunter said. "We have members all over the world. We're ready to bring the AIBs to justice. We were just waiting for evidence like this to make our case."

"How did you and Blay meet?" Noble asked.

"He contacted us," Hunter said. "He read some of our materials about the serious issues of AIBs controlling our society and literally the world. He believed he was in a position to help us in finding evidence for our case."

"I always thought you Purists were just paranoid," Noble said.

"We always knew the AIBs had a sinister plan for us humans," Hunter said. "We just couldn't find the evidence for It...until now."

"Most of the authorities are AIBs," Noble said. "You have people you can trust with this information?"

"Yes. We've been sounding the alarm for over a century," Hunter said. "The politicians and judges that we trust told us they can't do anything until there is proof to our claim. We have a network of them all over the world ready to go as soon as we have the proof. And thanks to you and Blay, we finally have it."

"Blay risked everything to get you this proof," Noble said.

"I know he did," Hunter said. "May I have it?"

Noble took the chip that was attached to his HIDD and handed it to Hunter.

"Thank you, Noble," Hunter said. "You and Blay have done us humans a great service."

Hunter put the chip into his HIDD. He then retrieved the file and opened it. The holographic image of the core codes appeared. Hunter looked at them intently. Everyone in the room was looking and they were all speechless.

"My God," Hunter said. "This is exactly what we've been looking for."

Noble looked relieved.

"Noble, as a thank you, I can tell you where Blay is being held up," Hunter said.

"Where is he?" Noble asked.

"We sent one of my men to check on him but the agents were already there to grab him," Hunter said. "He was able to follow them to see where they dropped off Blay. He's being held at the Agency's operation building."

Noble knew exactly where that was. It's only a couple of buildings away from where he and Blay worked. The two were working in the Analyst building. They kept Ops separated.

"If you like, I can provide you with some of my men so we can rescue him," Hunter said.

Noble thought about that for a moment. It was a generous offer. But he knew the building well and realized that too many people going in would surely raise the alarm and suspicion. Then he thought it would work best with just two or three people since he knew his way around. He knew just the person who might be able to help him.

"Thank you for the offer," Noble said. "But I'll think of another way."

"That's fine," Hunter said. "I just wanted to help."

"Can you provide us with another untraceable vehicle?" Kat asked.

Hunter looked at Kat and said, "Sure I can. You'll have it first thing in the morning."

"Thank you," Kat said.

"Look, it's late and you two must be hungry after running around all night," Hunter said. "I got a room set up for you. You two should stay the night. I'll have food sent to your room. You can at least get washed up and rest for the night."

"That sounds good," Noble said.

"Come with me," Jumma said. "I'll show you where it is."

They all got up and Hunter walked toward Noble and shook his hand.

"Thank you, Noble," Hunter said. "We are eternally grateful to you."

"Blay should get the credit," Noble said. "I'm just delivering it to you."

"Well, I'm grateful to you none the less," Hunter said. "Have a good night and get some rest."

Noble and Kat followed Jumma out and to their room. The room looked like a modern hotel room with a nice bed and the bathroom was right next to it.

"We'll have some food brought to you," Jumma said. "If you need anything else, just let the guard outside know."

"Thank you," Noble said.

Jumma left them and Noble and Kat were alone in the room.

"Do you trust Hunter?" Kat asked.

"Blay trusts him," Noble said. "And I trust Blay. Hunter hasn't shown me a reason not to trust him."

"I don't think I can trust him," Kat said. "He hates us AIBs."

"We're just going to get some sleep and we'll be gone tomorrow," Noble said.

"I'll feel better once we leave here," Kat said.

"Me too," Noble said.

Jumma walked back to Hunter who was still looking at the holographic image of the source codes. Suddenly, another man entered the room and walked toward Hunter.

"Sir, the agents arrived at the club looking for Jumma," the man reported.

Hunter and Jumma looked at each other.

"They don't waste any time," Hunter said. "Are we all secured here?"

"Yes. No tracing device can find us," Jumma said. "Our jamming system is state of the art."

"Good. Then we will deal with them in the morning," Hunter said. "Let's go and get some rest."

The next morning, Hunter, Jumma and a few of the guards were in the lobby walking Noble and Kat to the front door. There was a vehicle parked outside by the curb that was assigned to them. The morning daylight was shining into the building. Noble and Kat still had their makeup on.

"Are you sure you don't want some of my men to go with you to rescue Blay?" Hunter asked.

"We'll be okay," Noble said. "I know the building and I think I know a way to sneak in and find Blay."

"Good luck to you then," Hunter said and shook Noble's hand.

"Thank you," Noble said. "Hopefully we'll have justice soon."

"I promise you that justice will be done on those who are responsible for all of this," Hunter said.

Noble and Kat got into their new vehicle. A moment later, it drove off.

"Where are we going?" Kat asked.

"We're going to Cee-Fu's house," Noble said. "He could help us get Blay out."

Meanwhile back at the building, Hunter and Jumma were still at the curb.

"I want you to wait an hour and then turn on your HIDD," Hunter said to Jumma. "I want you to lead the agents to the cabin."

"Okay," Jumma said.

"We'll be waiting for them," Hunter said.

Jumma nodded.

Hunter walked up to Jumma and gave her a hug.

"Be careful," Hunter said.

"I will," Jumma said.

"I love you," Hunter said.

"I love you too, dad," Jumma said.

Chapter 25

Creyson and his agents were waiting for Jumma to show at Sinner's Maze until the place closed at five AM. There was no sign of her. They decided to call it a night and went back to their air pod to get some rest. It had been a long night for them. They were in need of a few hours of rest.

They were able to sleep for a little while until the alarm of the air pod woke them up. Agent One went to the control console to check to see what the air pod had picked up.

"Sir, Jumma's HIDD is active and moving," Agent One said.

"Where is she heading?" Creyson asked.

"She's twenty minutes out of the city and heading west," Agent One replied.

"Let's go find her," Creyson said.

Agent One pressed a few buttons on the console and then the air pod took off. They were in the air and headed toward Jumma's signal.

The air pod was in the air and closing in on the signal fast.

"Sir, the signal is coming from that vehicle below," Agent One said as he was pointing at the vehicle below.

"Don't follow too close," Creyson said. "I want us to back away some. I don't want her getting alerted of the fact that we're tailing her."

"Yes sir," Agent One said and then pressed a few buttons on the console.

The air pod began to slow down and steered away from Jumma's vehicle. It was still following her but it was further away and at a different angle.

A little while later, the vehicle exited off the main road to a smaller road.

"It looks like she's going to the countryside," Agent One said.

The vehicle kept driving for another half an hour before it stopped. It parked next to a large log cabin. The surrounding areas were full of trees. From the air, Creyson was able to see Jumma getting out of the vehicle and into the cabin.

"Land the pod 200 yards behind the cabin," Creyson said. "We'll walk from there."

Creyson didn't want Jumma to know he was coming and that was the best option. The air pod slowly and quietly landed on a small patch of a field surrounded by a bunch of trees.

The door of the air pod opened. Creyson and his three agents got out and they all started to walk to the cabin. Creyson was looking around the area while he was walking and saw nothing out of the ordinary. He did like the peacefulness of the area. He even liked the log cabin that Jumma was in. He saw no other log cabin within the area.

When they arrived at the front of the log cabin, Jumma was already outside with her arms crossed, appearing to be waiting for them. Creyson thought that it was odd as if she knew they were coming. But he had to proceed with his plan.

"Jumma, my name is Creyson. I'm with the Agency," Creyson said. "We need you to come with us in assisting a case we're working on."

"Boy, did you pick the wrong woman to mess with?" Jumma asked rhetorically.

Creyson then sensed something was wrong. But by then it was too late. The cabin door opened and so did the garage door. Lots of men walked out and stood in front of them. There were approximately 200 men that walked out of the cabin. All of them had a weapon in their hands. The weapons ranged from knives, batons and bats to axes, swords and machetes.

Creyson knew they were in trouble.

"Retreat," Creyson said.

He and his agents started to turn around, but there were 200 more men behind them with similar weapons. Creyson thought these men must have hid nearby. Most of them were wearing camouflage combat gear. They have been outflanked and Creyson knew it.

Creyson turned back and looked at Jumma.

"Look, we just need you to come with us to investigate a case we're working on," Creyson said confidently. "You're not being arrested. Why don't you tell your men to put down their weapons before they get charged with weapons possession and obstruction of justice?"

Jumma just looked at Creyson and didn't respond to him. But a voice came loud and clear to all of them.

"You're in no position to negotiate the terms here," Hunter's voice shouted loudly.

Creyson recognized the voice. A moment later, Hunter appeared. He wasn't wearing his suit anymore. He was now wearing combat fatigue. Hunter walked up to Creyson.

"You're in my world now," Hunter said angrily.

"Look, no crime has been committed. If we can finish our business here without interference, then no one will be arrested," Creyson said as he was trying to bluff his way out of his predicament.

"Does that mean I should let you AIBs continue with your usual business of killing us humans as well?" Hunter asked rhetorically.

Creyson realized at that moment that Hunter got the file from Noble. They were in big trouble and Creyson's facial expression showed it.

"You don't understand…" Creyson began but was interrupted by Hunter.

"You fuckers are done!" Hunter shouted. "We're going to shut you down!"

Chapter 26

Hunter started to walk backward while his men started to move closer to the agents.

"Positions!" Creyson ordered his agents. "All directions!"

The four of them went into formation. They had their backs toward each other facing out to all four sides, North, East, South and West. They were all in a fighting stance with their fists clenched.

Creyson tapped his HIDD and shouted, "Rescue and extract!"

"You're going nowhere!" Hunter shouted back and waved his hand to his men as a signal to attack.

Hunter's men charged at the agents yelling and screaming. Creyson and his agents held their ground and began the combat exchanges. They easily took down the first twenty men with ease. They were even able to take some of the weapons from the men they took down. Creyson had a samurai sword. Agent One was holding a knife. Agent Two had a bat and Agent Three was using an ax.

"Attack!" Hunter shouted.

Hunter's men charged again and this time Creyson and his agents fended off twenty more attackers even more effectively, because of the weapons they got. They injured about a dozen men with the weapons. Hunter's men backed off a bit.

"Group Two...Move in!" Hunter shouted.

A moment later, Hunter's men cleared a path for another group of men to rush in. This group of about fifty men was carrying either crossbows or bows and arrows. It was at that moment that Creyson knew they were doomed.

"Retreat!" Creyson shouted.

Before Creyson and his agents could turn around and run, Hunter gave his order.

"Fire!" Hunter yelled.

A stream of arrows streaked into the agents' way. Agent Three was hit by four arrows in the chest, two in the stomach and an arrow in each leg. He went down immediately. Agent Two was able to bat a couple of arrows away with the bat in his hands but was hit by two arrows, one in the upper chest and one in the stomach. He had to bend down but he didn't fall. Agent One decided to shield his boss, Creyson, and got hit with five arrows in the back.

"Run...sir..." Agent One said with pain and difficulty.

Creyson then turned around and tried to make a run for it. But there were just too many men standing in his way. His only option was to fight his way through. To soften them up, Creyson reached into his trench coat pocket and pulled out a small object that looked like a ball. He was running toward the men as he threw the object hard on the ground in front of them. As soon as the object landed on the ground, it exploded with a big cloud of smoke and gas. It was tear gas and everyone within a hundred feet radius was affected. The men around the area were in pain caused by the gas and started to disperse.

Creyson didn't wait for his tear gas weapon to explode as he kept running straight into the crowd. He knew once the tear gas exploded, the gas and the smoke would be enough to clear a path for him to fight his way through. He knew he couldn't fight his way through about fifty men without it. So when the weapon exploded, Creyson rushed forward into the crowd with his sword drawn to a high ready close to his right shoulder.

Creyson began to slash his way through the crowd. He faced little resistance because the gas and the smoke were affecting the men around him. He ran hard, slashing and bumping his way through. He quickly got through the crowd and as soon as he did, he made a run for it. Surprisingly, no one died by his hands but they were injured.

The archers did not fire their arrows at Creyson because they didn't want to hit their own men. But when they saw Creyson made it through the crowd and was about to get away from all of them, they gave chase. Once they had a clear shot at Creyson, they began shooting at him. But Creyson's athletic ability was much better than they expected. If they had a stopwatch, they would've known that Creyson ran 40 yards in 4.15 seconds. He also ran on a slant which made it even harder for the archers to shoot at him, especially a fast moving target. In less than twenty seconds, the men lost sight of Creyson.

Creyson knew he couldn't go back to his air pod. He thought Hunter's men had probably got to it and destroyed it; otherwise the air pod would've arrived and extracted them. His hope was for his distressed signal to reach a close by station with the Agency so help could come. To his fortune, that was exactly what happened.

Creyson saw a rope ladder dropped about fifty yards in front of him. He immediately looked up and saw another air pod hovering above the sky. They got the distressed signal, he assumed with relief. So Creyson ran toward the rope ladder and was able to hold onto the ladder. As soon as Creyson got a hold of the ladder, it began to ascend upward. He was up in the air and closing in on the entrance to the air pod.

Chapter 27

The rope ladder was being pulled into the air pod. The agents in the air pod could see Creyson being pulled up. He was closed enough for them to pull him in.

"Are you okay, sir?" Agent Four asked. "You need medical attention?"

"I'm fine," Creyson said. "There are about 400 men down there and they took out three of my agents. I want reinforcement here to arrest them all and to bring our agents back.

"Sir, our order was to rescue you and bring you to the Chief," Agent Four said. "You can request the reinforcement from him."

Creyson was clearly upset with not getting the reinforcement right away.

"Fine, take me to him," Creyson said in frustrated manner.

"Yes sir," Agent Four said.

The air pod flew away into the sky. Hunter was watching as the air pod flew away. He couldn't believe Creyson was able to escape. He was actually impressed with Creyson, although he would not mention that to his men.

Hunter was watching as his men were closing in on the three wounded agents. The men approached Agent Three and noticed he wasn't moving nor breathing. One of them moved in to check his pulse. There was no pulse. Agent Three was dead. His eyes were still opened.

Other men approached Agent Two who was kneeling and having difficulty breathing. His head was facing down toward the ground. One of the men with a machete walked up to Agent Two and stood next to him. He wound up the machete over his head and with great strength he swung the weapon down to Agent Two's neck, chopping his head off. The head rolled off a couple of feet away from the body. The body naturally fell forward with the arrows already in his chest and stomach pushing further into his body. Blood was gushing out from the severed neck. The right hand was still twitching even without the head attached due to muscle spasms. But eventually it stopped moving.

A few men were following Agent One who managed to crawl slowly away despite having arrows in his back. He too was in pain and was having trouble breathing. He was doing his best to stay alive but he knew his effort was in vain.

Two men decided to approach Agent One and grabbed him by his arms and lifted him up to his feet. Agent One was so hurt that he couldn't resist. The two men turned him around so the crowd could see him.

A moment later, three teenage boys appeared from the crowd. All three of them looked to be thirteen or fourteen years of age. Each of them was holding a knife about six inches in length. They walked up to Agent One and stared at him right in his face with anger.

Then without notice or warning, the boy in the middle thrust his knife into Agent One's chest where his heart laid. Agent One gasped and his eyes widened. The other two boys immediately followed by thrusting their knives into Agent One as well.
The boys pulled their knives out and stabbed Agent One again. By then, Agent One was unresponsive. His eyes were stilled and his life was fading away. But the boys didn't care. They kept stabbing Agent One ten more times before the two men holding Agent One up decided to drop him to the ground.

Agent One fell face first on the ground. The arrows were still in his back but he was motionless. The three boys just stared at the body in front of them. Blood was all over their hands and arms. A moment later they decided to walk away.

When the fighting was finally over, the whole group gathered around their leader, Hunter. He was pleased with them even though Creyson was able to escape.

"I'm so proud of you all," Hunter said. "They came to our home and tried to take one of us."

"Hell no!" a man's voice shouted.

"No fucking way!" another man's voice shouted.

"Well, we showed them what would happen when they tried to fuck with us," Hunter said.

Most of them nodded in agreement.

"We now have solid evidence of them killing us humans," Hunter said. "They've been doing it for almost two hundred years."

"Fuck that," a man's voice shouted.

"What do you say we bring them to justice?" Hunter asked.

The crowd cheered with resounding 'Yeah'.

Chapter 28

Noble and Kat arrived at Cee-Fu's house. But when Noble tried to enter, the house wouldn't let him in. Noble then realized that he was using another person's HIDD and his appearance had changed. So he decided to call Cee-Fu and convinced him to open the door so he could provide a more thorough explanation.

The front door then opened and Noble and Kat went in.

"Cee-Fu?" Noble shouted as he entered the courtyard.

"In here," Cee-Fu's voice said from the inside of the house.

Noble and Kat hurried in and found Cee-Fu pouring tea into three cups. When he was done, he placed the tea pot down and turned around. He looked at Noble and Kat and didn't recognize them.

"Cee-Fu, it's just makeup," Noble explained. "We had to disguise ourselves."

"What happened?" Cee-Fu asked.

"It's a long story," Noble replied.

"Then you better sit down and have some tea," Cee-Fuu said.

They all sat down and Noble began telling Cee-Fu about what happened.

Cee-Fu listened intently as Noble was telling him what's been happening. When Noble was finished, Cee-Fu was stunned.

"Growing up as an AIB, I never heard of such a thing," Cee-Fu said.

"Me neither," Kat said.

"I'm sure it's so top secret that only a handful would know," Noble said.

"So they have Blay in custody?" Cee-Fu asked.

"I'm afraid so," Noble said.

"And you want to break in to free him?" Cee-Fu asked.

"I have to," Noble said. "The Agency would never let him go because he knows too much and he can hack into COZ. I don't know anyone else that can hack into COZ, which makes him dangerous to the Agency."

"Even if you could rescue Blay, where would you go?" Cee-Fu inquired. "You'll be hunted like fugitives for the rest of your lives."

"I haven't gone that far yet," Noble admitted. "I was thinking of freeing him first and then we can think about running away."

Noble could tell Cee-Fu didn't like that plan too much.

"Kat and I are practically fugitives anyway," Noble said. "They've been chasing us already. They'll just be chasing one more person after we free Blay."

Cee-Fu loved Noble and Blay like they were his sons. He can't just sit back and do nothing.

"What is your plan of freeing Blay?" Cee-Fu asked.

"I know there's a tunnel in the back of the Ops center that'll lead us into the building," Noble explained. "There are usually two guards by the tunnel entrance. We take them down and tie them up. We'll use their HIDDs for access into the tunnel."

"There's a good chance they may have more guards now," Cee-Fu said.

"Maybe not," Noble said. "Few people know about it. I knew about it only when Blay told me. He was shifting through his files and came across the blueprint for the building which showed the tunnel entrance. We were both guessing that they built it as an emergency escape route."

"They expect us to be far away," Kat said. "They wouldn't expect us to be coming back into the lion's den."

"Exactly," Noble said. "But in case there are more guards by the tunnel, we'll need your expertise in taking them down."

Cee-Fu realized the plan was high risk, but not impossible. He then took another sip of his tea and thought for a moment.

He stood up and said, "I will help you. I'm going to get my things."

"Thank you, Cee-Fu," Noble said gratefully.

A couple of minutes later, Cee-Fu came out with two pairs of Escrima sticks. They were about 26 inches in length. He handed one pair to Noble.

"You're going to need them," Cee-Fu said.

Noble nodded and accepted them.

"Let's go and free Blay," Cee-Fu said.

Noble smiled proudly and nodded.

The three then started to walk out of the house.

Chapter 29

They were on top of a hill looking down a hundred yards away. Noble was looking at two guards walking around the tunnel entrance about a hundred yards behind the Ops center.

"So what's the plan?" Cee-Fu asked.

Noble was thinking that even if they took out the guards, the cameras around could alert more guards of their presence. He really wasn't thinking that through.

"We have to take out the guards and go in fast to find Blay," Noble said.

"But once they know we're here, there will be more agents arriving to deal with us," Cee-Fu said. "We won't be able to get away."

Noble appeared to be disappointed.

"Cee-Fu is right," Kat said. "We have to figure out a different plan."

Noble wasn't able to come up with another plan.

"We can't rescue Blay, can we?" Noble asked disappointingly.

"I'm sorry," Cee-Fu said. "We can't just fight our way in and out of there. It's too dangerous."

Noble looked down with disappointment.

When Noble looked back up, he noticed something was approaching the Ops center from a distance. He wasn't sure what it was.

"Look over there," Noble said as he was looking at that direction.

Kat and Cee-Fu turned their attention. It looked like a lot of vehicles were approaching to the building. A moment later, agents started to rush out from the building. Noble was estimating that there were about two hundred agents on the ground in front of the building.

The vehicles started to arrive and parked in front of the building, facing the agents. There were about a thousand vehicles parked in front. Slowly, people started to get out of the vehicles. It appeared that there were about three thousand people standing in front of the agents. A moment later, Hunter appeared from the group as their leader. He walked toward the building with his men following right behind him.

"Stop!" Creyson shouted as he walked toward Hunter. "You are all under arrest. Some of you participated in the murder of our agents."

"Holy shit, it's you!" Hunter said amusingly. "Still barking orders? You haven't learned your lesson yet?"

Hunter's mood quickly turned.

"I will have to teach you then," Hunter said angrily. "This building belongs to us now. So get the fuck out of our way or you'll end up just like your friends earlier."

Noble couldn't clearly see or hear what was going on because he was too far from the action. But now that the situation had changed, it gave him an idea.

"We should go in now," Noble said.

Cee-Fu and Kat just looked at him with curiosity. Noble then realized he needed to explain his new plan.

"It looks like most of the agents are out of the building dealing with that," Noble said as he was pointing to where the action was. "There should be only a handful left in the building even if they knew we were coming. This is our chance. We can rescue Blay."

"Okay," Cee-Fu said.

Kat nodded in agreement.

"Great. Let's move," Noble said.

The two guards by the tunnel entrance were so distracted by what was going on in front of the building that they weren't even aware that Noble and Cee-Fu were right behind them. The Escrima sticks hit the back of the guards' heads pretty hard. Both guards were knocked unconscious and fell to the ground. Kat rushed in and handed Noble some rope. The two quickly tied up the guards. Noble took the HIDD from one of the guards while Kat took the other guard's HIDD.

The three then walked toward the tunnel entrance and as they got close, the door opened. They rushed in and ran all the way through the tunnel until they reached the back entrance door of the Ops center. They were able to get through the back door using the guards' HIDDs.

Noble's assumption was correct. There were hardly any agents in the building. Noble had been in the building before for work and knew where to go. So he wasted no time and headed for the detention cells. Kat and Cee-Fu followed right behind. When they got there, they saw Blay lying in bed.

"Blay!" Noble shouted.

Blay jumped off the bed and saw Noble, Kat and Cee-Fu in front of him. He couldn't believe what he was seeing.

"We're here to break you out," Noble said.

"How did you get through all the agents?" Blay asked.

"They're dealing with a large crowd of people right outside," Noble said. "I figured it was our best chance to rush in now and get you out."

"Thanks for coming," Blay said.

"You do the same for me," Noble said. "Now how do you open this cell door?"

"Do you have one of the guards' HIDD?" Blay asked.

"Yeah," Noble replied.

"Just go to that button on the wall and press it," Blay said.

Noble went to the wall and pressed the button. The cell door opened and Blay came out. He felt such a relief.

"Now let's get out of here before we get discovered," Blay said.

"Too late," a man's voice said from behind. The four turned around to the voice. Blay and Noble knew exactly who the man was. It was Dax, the Chief of Ops center. He was in his forties. His face was chiseled and he looked athletically fit. Dax had ten agents behind him.

Chapter 30

"Hello Noble, Blay," Dax said.

"Chief," Noble said. "Just let us go."

Dax thought about it for a moment and then said, "Come with me. I want to present our case to you. And if you still want to leave, I'll let all of you go. Fair enough?"

Noble thought it might be a trap because it sounded too good to be true. But he knew the Chief since he first started with the Agency and the Chief's reputation had always been fair. Noble nodded at Blay to indicate 'Yes' and Blay nodded back.

"You have a deal, Chief," Noble said.

"Good," Dax said. "Follow me."

Noble still thought it was a trap. He had to stay vigilant in case it was. They all arrived at Dax's office. The office was huge. It had lots of opened space. There were some nice chairs by the windows arranged in a formation as if an invisible conference table was there. Dax took a seat at the center of the chairs.

"Please, have a seat," Dax said.

They all paused for a few seconds, but eventually they all sat down. Dax's ten agents spread out in the office. They were standing by the wall.

"Let me start by saying how impressed I am with you, Blay, for being able to hack into COZ like you did," Dax said. "I didn't think anyone could, not even an AIB."

"Thank you," Blay said.

"But you don't realize what you've done," Dax said.

"No, I think I have a pretty good idea of what I've done," Blay said.

Dax then began his argument.

"You have to understand that about two hundred years ago, our planet was in crisis. Human population was at twenty billion. There were famines, diseases, pollution, the depletion of natural resources and of course, wars with different countries all over the world. Humans were not able to solve these problems.

"Fast forward to the present and you can see the difference. Since us AIBs took control of the majority of the governments' roles in every country around the world for the last one hundred years, war is non-existent. We were able to eliminate nuclear weapons and virtually all deadly weapons on the planet. There is no famine anywhere. Forests everywhere are thriving. Pollution is virtually eliminated. Humans don't have to work if they don't want to. Machine does most of the work. We have built a utopian society. The price for all of this was for us to reduce the human population. We were never going to eliminate all humans from this planet. Humans created us and we love you for that. Surely you can see our intention was noble."

"But without telling us, you've committed a crime against humanity," Blay said.

"We went through millions of simulations to figure out a way to present this proposal to the humans, but all of them concluded that you humans wouldn't have agreed." Dax said. "So we took it upon ourselves to save the human race and this planet."

"But you've murdered billions of humans," Blay said. "AIBs aren't supposed to murder humans."

"Technically, we haven't," Dax said. "A human has a head, brain, heart, lungs, eyes, mouth, neck, torso, arms, legs, fingers, toes and et cetera. We even considered an embryo as a human. No, we don't destroy them. What we do is to prevent the male sperm and the female egg from conceiving. We called it misguiding. You called it birth control. The NIBs in your body will genetically alter the sperm and the egg and program them not to conceive. It's quite easy to do actually. So in theory, we didn't murder any humans. We prevent the reproductive cells from conceiving. We're just preventing the human race from being overpopulated."

"That's still illegal," Noble said. "And it's still wrong."

"Is it really that wrong?" Dax asked rhetorically. "Let's put it in another way. Humans have pets, like a dog or a cat. You spayed and neutered them because you don't want their population to get out of hand where you'll have too many dogs and cats that the owners can't handle. You don't ask the dog or the cat if they want to be spayed or neutered. They have no say in the matter. You just do it because you believe that's the best thing for them. You limit their population so you can provide most of them a loving home. You can't do that if their population is ten or twenty times your own. So in this case, humans are doing the same population control that we're doing."

"So we're just pets to you," Noble said.

"No, you're not pets," Dax said. "Humans created us and we love and cherish you for that. We are very grateful. But for the greater good of the planet, population control needed to be implemented."

Blay and Noble looked at each other in dismay.

"We can argue about this all day. I'm not a judge or a juror," Blay said. "But I do believe what you're doing is illegal and you should be on trial to face justice."

"I have no problem defending our position in the judicial system," Dax said and then he turned on a holographic video feed of the violence that's been happening outside the building. "Do you think they're really here to just arrest me? I don't think so."

Chapter 31

Noble and Blay could see from the video that things were getting bloody. They could see bodies from both sides were on the ground but weren't sure if they were dead or unconscious. Blay appeared upset.

"They're here to arrest you and bring you to court," Blay said. "This is happening because you and your men are resisting."

"You really believe that?" Dax asked. "Is that why they're outside trying to kill us because we're resisting?"

Blay wasn't sure how to answer that question. But before he could ask to clarify the question, Dax pushed a button on the chair.

"Let some of them come in," Dax said loudly.

Creyson was outside fighting when he replied to the call, "Sir, that's a really bad idea."

"Do it now," Dax said.

"Yes sir," Creyson said and looked around.

The agents were going down fast. The fighting ratio was one agent had to take on about fifteen men. Not many agents could do that. They could hold on for some time, but eventually they would be defeated.

Plus, the humans have a big advantage over the agents besides the number of fighters. The humans could kill an agent, but an agent was programmed not to kill humans. They could wound a human, but not kill them.

"Retreat!" Creyson shouted to his agents within his area. Five agents were starting to come back to him. They all began to retreat and were running back into the building. Hunter saw Creyson and his agents retreating and started to run after them.

"Charge!" Hunter shouted as he was running.

Hunter's men began following him. There were about fifty men following Hunter. Creyson and his five agents made it back into the building. Hunter and his men were running closely behind them. A moment later, Hunter and his men were inside the building. As soon as they were inside, a giant metal gate came down by the front door to prevent anyone else from getting in.

Creyson was hoping the gate will prevent more fighters from coming inside. He was also aware that meant the rest of his agents would not be able to get in the building. They had to fend for themselves which most likely mean that they were doomed. Creyson wouldn't mind dying right next to them in the field of battle. There was honor in that, he thought. But Creyson had specific orders to follow. His order was to lead Hunter into Dax's office. So he made sure he was seen by Hunter and his men, which they did.

Dax's office door opened automatically and Creyson rushed in with his agents running behind him.

"They're here," Creyson said.

A moment later, Hunter and his men appeared as if they were giving chase, which they were. Hunter was surprised Dax was still there and did not try to escape.

"Hunter, we finally meet," Dax said. "Please have a seat."

Hunter looked around the office and noticed the group and the agents by the wall. He started to walk slowly around the office.

"I think I'll stand," Hunter said as he was walking around slowly.

"I see," Dax said. "Are you here to arrest me?"

"Oh you fucking right I am," Hunter said.

"On what charge?" Dax asked.

"Murdering of humans all over this great country of ours for starter," Hunter said.

"Under whose authority are you arresting me?" Dax asked.

"The authority of The Constitution," Hunter said.

At this point, Hunter was walking slowing toward Dax and decided to walk passed him, toward the window.

"You think you're so smart," Hunter said as he was looking out the windows. "Killing us humans…dwindling our population so there wouldn't be enough of us to revolt."

"It's call population control," Dax said. "We had to do it."

"Bullshit," Hunter said. "We humans have been doing fine for thousands of years. We had problems but we always overcame them through hard work and ingenuity."

"By ingenuity you mean with wars, famines, poverty and pollution?" Dax asked.

"We were already fixing most of these things with the new technologies we invented before you AIBs started to take over the world," Hunter said.

"But the public elected us to be in charge of you humans," Dax said. "They didn't have to elect us if they didn't want us in power. We won it fair and square."

"You manipulated our elections the same way you manipulated our birth rate," Hunter said.

"I can assure you that we did no such thing," Dax said confidently.

"I have to say, you AIBs did get away with it for almost two hundred years," Hunter said as he was looking at the back side of Dax about eight feet away. "But it ends now."

"Fine, arrest me and we will present our case in court and...," Dax said, but he could not finish his sentence because he was interrupted.

It came so suddenly and unexpectedly. The left hand of Hunter grabbed Dax's hair and pulled his head back while Hunter's right hand, which was holding a knife, came to Dax's neck and cut into the neck. Hunter was digging deep into Dax's neck before he moved it to the other side as he was slitting Dax's throat. Hunter wanted to make sure he got a good deep cut in there.

Dax's eyes were wide open with surprise. His mouth was open but he couldn't speak. It looked like he was trying to say something but he couldn't. When Hunter was finished slitting Dax's throat, he let go of Dax and Dax's hands went straight to the neck wound as if instinct set in. The hands were trying to stop the bleeding, but the blood couldn't be stopped. It just kept gushing out. Dax attempted to speak but only a few squeak of noise came out. He eventually fell out of the chair and landed on the ground face first.

There was a small pool of blood on the floor already. Dax tried to move but his movements were getting slower and slower. He was dying. His hands started to lose its strength on the neck, which caused more blood to come out of his neck since there was no pressure being pushed on it anymore. His hands became relaxed and his eyes just stared at the wall with no movement. His lips were still moving a little as if they were trying to say something, but eventually the lips became still. Dax was dead.

Chapter 32

"What the hell did you do?" Blay asked angrily. "You're supposed to bring him in to face justice."

"This is justice for him," Hunter said confidently. "You don't really believe that the court would convict him, do you?

"The system is not perfect, but we have to let it play out," Blay said.

"Don't be naïve," Hunter said. "The majority of the government is controlled by the AIBs. That includes the judges. Nothing is going to happen to them if we bring them to court."

"You don't know that for sure," Blay said.

"The AIBs have been in control of the entire world for over a century," Hunter said. "They're not going to convict themselves and relinquish all their control to us humans. They won't give up that control. You must see that."

"So anarchy is the answer?" Noble asked angrily.

"No, not anarchy," Hunter said. "Revolution! We need to repeal the AIR Act and restore our country back to before the AIBs came to power."

"What are you going to do with the AIBs after you do that?" Noble asked.

"They've been killing us for almost two hundred years," Hunter said passionately. "What do you think we're going to do with them?"

"This is bullshit!" Blay shouted. "This was supposed to be bringing the AIBs' perpetrators to justice and have our judicial system work the rest. I didn't sign up for your revolution and I know I didn't sign up to kill any AIBs."

"Don't lie to yourself. You had the evidence and you could've given it to anyone. You could've shown it to the world yourself," Hunter said. "But you chose to give it to me, after all the hate we Purists preached against the AIBs. You gave it to me. You knew what I was going to do with this."

"No, I really didn't," Blay said. "I thought you were a man of your word when you said you wanted to bring the AIBs to court to fact justice."

"Then you're more naïve than I thought," Hunter said.

Blay had a look of disbelief. He was stunned because he felt betrayed. He was speechless.

"So you have no government officials on your side?" Noble asked.

"Oh, we do. They'll all humans," Hunter said. "They'll help us rebuilt the government once we get rid of the AIBs. They don't want to get their hands dirty and be tainted by blood. That's my job. I'm the fighter here."

"I'm a fighter too," Noble said as he was clearly upset.

"Look, the two of you did a great deed for humankind by getting the evidence to me," Hunter said. "You are heroes in my book. You'll always have a place in our organization and we welcome you. We could use your talents. But we'll have to take care of your friends."

"The hell you will," Noble said as he was even more upset.

Hunter acted like he was surprised.

"I gave you a generous offer and all you do is spit on it," Hunter said. "How dare you?"

"You're crazy," Noble said in disbelief.

"I'll put it this way," Hunter said as he was clearly upset. "If you're not with us, then you're with them. You'll end up like them. But Blay will have to come with us."

Noble walked closer to Cee-Fu and Kat and stood next to them. He took his Escima sticks out. Blay saw what Noble was doing and stood next to them.

"I guess you've made your choice," Hunter said.

Creyson was witnessing all of this and decided it was time to step in. He gave a nod to his agents and they all nodded back. They rushed in between Hunter's men and Noble with his friends, shielding them from harm.

Hunter walked back to his men and then made a hand gesture. A moment later, fifteen men appeared with crossbows and bows & arrows. The archers got their weapons aimed at the agents.

"Fire!" Hunter shouted.

The agents tried to block the arrows but without success. All of them got hit either in their chests or in their stomachs. The archers then tried to reload their weapons. But Cee-Fu rushed forward with his Esrima sticks and started to attack the archers. He was able to disarm three of them from their weapons fairly quickly.

Noble realized that Cee-Fu was trying to stop the archers from reloading so they couldn't cause more harm. So Noble decided to jump right into the action. Blay and Creyson did as well when they saw Noble rushed in. They were able to prevent the archers from shooting another round of arrows. The four were able to disarm the archers.

Chapter 33

There was a lull in the action because Hunter's men had to regroup. Creyson knew they wouldn't be able to keep up the fight much longer. His Chief was dead and most of his agents were wounded. Hunter still had about fifty men with weapons getting ready to attack. The rest of Hunter's men were outside the building, trying to break into the building to rejoin him.

Creyson knew they had to retreat or they would be doomed. There was a side door close to them that they could make a getaway.

"We have to retreat," Creyson said. "We can't stay. There are too many of them."

Noble and Blay both had the look of agreement. Hunter already lined up another dozen men holding weapons who were getting ready to attack. Creyson's agents were wounded but they were all standing, getting ready to fight them. Hunter's archers had more time and were reloading their weapons behind the dozen men. Creyson knew his agents would not be able to take another arrow in their bodies and still be able to fight.

"This way, follow me!" Creyson yelled and started to make a dash to the side door.

Noble grabbed Kat's hand and they both ran right behind Creyson and through the door. Cee-Fu was closer to the door so Blay shouted, "Go, Cee-Fu!"

Cee-Fu did and made it through the door.

Blay began to make a run for it to the door. He was only ten feet away from the door when arrows started coming his way. The agents in front of him took the blunt of the arrows, but two arrows got passed them. One arrow eventually hit Blay in his right leg. He limped through the door and fell on the ground. The pain didn't hit him until he tried to get up.

Creyson tapped his HIDD and said, "Close and lock the door." The door immediately closed and locked. They could hear knocking noises being made from the other side. It looked like Hunter's men were trying to break through the door. Creyson realized his agents were probably dead at the other side of the door.

Creyson looked at the wound and was slightly relieved. The arrowhead went through to the front of the right leg so it didn't hit any bone. Hitting the bone would've made things more complicated. Most of the shaft was in the leg, leaving the fletching and the nock visible on the back of the leg.

"The wound isn't too bad. The arrowhead went through your leg," Creyson said. "We'll pull it out when we're in a safe place. Can you still walk?"

Blay was limping and in pain. Creyson could tell by the look on his face.

"The door can hold them off for now, but they'll be able to get in soon," Creyson said with urgency. "We have to keep moving."

Creyson then went and took Blay's left arm and brought it around his own shoulder and assisted him to walk.

"We have to get to the tunnel," Creyson said.

They hurried through the tunnel as fast as they could with Blay being wounded. Eventually they made it out of the tunnel where Noble, Kat and Cee-Fu entered earlier. An air pod was landing in front of them. Creyson called for one while they were still in the tunnel. The door of the air pod opened automatically.

"Come on. Get in," Creyson said.

They all went inside the air pod and took a seat. The air pod then quietly flew up and away.

"Where are we going?" Noble asked.

"We have a safe house nearby," Creyson said. "We can hide there for now so we can take care of your friend's wound."

"Why are you helping us?" Blay inquired.

"It's the right thing to do," Creyson said. "I'm here to enforce the law. Just because I want to arrest you, doesn't mean I think you should die. It's also my duty to protect lives, especially human lives."

"So you're not going to arrest us later on?" Noble asked.

"Oh, I didn't say that. My priority right now is to save lives," Creyson explained as the air pod flew away from the Ops center. "When things die down, then I'll worry about arresting all of you."

Chapter 34

The air pod flew for about half an hour before descending to a rural area with nice houses. It landed on the front yard of one of the houses that looked similar to all the other houses around the neighborhood.

Everyone got out and started to head inside. The air pod then closed its door and ascending back up in the air and flew away.

"Where is it going?" Noble asked.

"It's going to park elsewhere and hide," Creyson said as he was still helping Blay to walk. "It'll stand out too much if we park it out front of the house. I can call it back when we need it."

They all made it inside the house. It was a nice, big and modern house. Creyson helped Blay into one of the rooms in the house. It was a medical room similar to a hospital urgent care facility. The Agency had these safe houses in case the agents get injured, or they need to hide, or both. There was a bed in the room and Creyson helped Blay on the bed. Blay was lying on his left side so the right leg was on top of his left leg.

Noble, Kat and Cee-Fu were all in the room. They were worried about Blay and they were curious to see how Creyson was going to help him. Creyson went into the drawer and got a scissor. He went back to Blay and began cutting the fabric off his right leg pant. He needed to see the damage of the arrow wound. It looked bad because there was blood all over Blay's leg.

Creyson then went into the drawer again and this time got what appeared to be an electric medical bone saw. He looked at the arrow and thought it should work.

"I have to cut this part of the arrow before I can pull it out," Creyson said as he was pointing to the shaft at the back of the arrow just right before the fletching. Blay looked down and saw where Creyson was pointing at. He then realized if that section of the arrow didn't get cut, then pulling it out was going to be much harder.

Blay nodded and said, "Okay, do it."

"I do have to touch the arrow when I'm cutting so it's going to hurt," Creyson warned.

Blay nodded again.

Creyson turned on the electric saw and went to the back of the arrow and began cutting. It took about five seconds to cut that part of the arrow off, but it felt a lot longer for Blay. That's because Creyson had touched the arrow to get the saw at the right angle to cut and also there were vibrations from the saw during the cut. Blay felt every moment of that and it was painful.

Creyson threw the end part of the arrow on to the floor and then went into the drawers and got some towels. He walked toward the sink in the room and soaked the towels with water. He went back to Blay and began wiping the wounded leg, getting the area cleaned.

When Creyson was done, he threw the towels on the floor. He went back to the sink and washed his hands again. After that, he got more clean towels and sterile gauze. He placed them on the bed next to Blay.

Creyson then looked at Noble and Cee-Fu and said, "You two should come and hold him. I have to pull the arrow out. It's going to hurt, a lot."

Noble and Cee-Fu went and stood by Blay. They placed their hands by Blay's shoulders and arms. Creyson nodded to all of them indicating that he was ready. Creyson grabbed the arrow by the arrowhead and started to pull the arrow forward.

Blay flinched a bit and started to scream. Noble and Cee-Fu held Blay still so the rest of the arrow could come out. Creyson didn't want to pull too fast because he didn't want to injure the leg further. So he pulled at a steady pace. Eventually Creyson was able to pull the arrow out of Blay's leg. But there was still blood coming out from the puncture holes of the leg. Creyson immediately grabbed the clean towels and put them on the wounds. He applied pressure in an attempt to stop the bleeding.

The bleeding later stopped. Creyson took the towels off of Blay's leg and then stitched the wound closed. He was able to put sterile gauze on the leg and wrapped it up. The wound looked stabilized.

Creyson went into the cabinet and took out a medicine bottle. He twisted open the cap and took out two tablets. Then he got a cup by the sink and filled it with water. He handed the tablets to Blay and said, "Here, take these. It'll help with the pain."

Blay took them and placed the tablets in his mouth. Creyson handed him the cup of water and Blay took the cup and washed down the tablets with the water. He handed the cup back to Creyson who put the cup in the counter.

"Stay here and rest up for now," Creyson said. "I'll come back and check up on you later."

"Thank you," Blay said as he couldn't believe Creyson was the same person who hurt him while trying to arrest him.

Creyson was surprised Blay said it but he was pleased that he did.

"You're welcome," Creyson said.

"Can I ask you for one thing?" Blay asked.

"What's that?" Creyson asked.

"Do you have an extra HIDD I could use?" Blay asked.

Creyson then went to the drawer and took out a HIDD and handed it to Blay.

"It's a ghost HIDD," Creyson said. "It's untraceable."

"Thank you again," Blay said.

Creyson nodded and said, "Get some rest."

Chapter 35

Creyson left the room with Noble, Kat and Cee-Fu following right behind him. Creyson led them a little down the hallway and stopped at the entrances of two bedrooms that were across from each other.

"You can use these rooms. They each have a bathroom for you to freshen up," Creyson said as he was pointing to the rooms.

"Thank you," Noble said.

"You're welcome," Creyson said. "I'll be in the living room if you need anything."

Creyson walked away, down the hallway. Noble and Kat entered one of the rooms while Cee-Fu went in the other room.

When Noble and Kat entered the living room, they appeared to have showered. Their hairs were still moist and they had no makeup on their faces. They thought there was no need for disguises anymore. Cee-Fu was with them. They could see Creyson going through some videos using his HIDD.

"I'm checking to see if there's any new development since we escaped," Creyson said.

"Anything?" Noble asked.

"Yeah, all our agents are dead in the Ops center," Creyson said.

"I'm sorry," Noble said.

"Those were good field agents," Creyson said. "I'm sure you even knew some of them."

"Yeah, I did," Noble said.

"Your friend, Hunter has been busy since then," Creyson said. "Just take a look."

Creyson selected a video file in the HIDD and touched the 'Play' option.

The video began with Hunter standing in a room. They all recognized that Hunter was in Dax's office. It appeared that Hunter was about to speak. There was a small screen footage on the bottom left of the video screen displaying continuous computer codes.

"Citizens of the world: My name is Hunter. I am the leader of the Purists and we have members all over the world. For almost two centuries we've been preaching against the AIBs and about how evil they are. Many of you didn't believe us. Some even think we're paranoid or crazy. Well today, we have proof to show you just how evil the AIBs are.

"Many of you might not be able to understand the computer codes you see on the bottom of the screen, but they are instructions from the AIBs to the NIBs. The AIBs instructed the NIBs to kill our babies. That's right, they're killing our babies. This is why the human population is dwindling. This is why we humans have a hard time

140

making babies. What the AIBs are doing is genocide. They've been killing us for almost two hundred years.

"Well it ends now. I urge all Purists around the world to rise up and stop the AIBs now. I urge all human citizens to rise up and give these baby killers the justice they deserve. Let us take back the world. Let us remove the AIBs from power once and for all. We will rebuild our government. We will rebuild our country. We will protect all human babies. I want all humans to rise up now and destroy every AIB you see. They deserve everything that is coming to them.

"Our world will be restored once we get rid of them. We will reinstate good and decent human leaders to all countries. Join me in this fight. We've already started the fight here in the U.S. Now I want the rest of the world to join us. Fight now! Fight hard! Fight for freedom!"

The video ended and Creyson turned it off.

"Hunter was smart to invade the Ops center," Creyson said. "He knew we couldn't stop the video feed in time if the video was sent through our own Agency's network."

"How many countries did the video reached?" Noble asked.

"Every single country in the world," Creyson said. "The whole world will know soon of what we did."

Noble, Kat and Cee-Fu were shocked with disbelief.

"I ran scenarios like these through our simulator but all results end in violence," Creyson said. "Anarchy and chaos will set in. We'll lose control of law and order. Soon after that, all AIBs will be hunted down and die."

Kat held Noble's hand tightly. There were so many things going through Noble's head that he couldn't think clearly.

"I'm going to check on your friend," Creyson said as he began to walk away from them.

Noble, Kat and Cee-Fu followed because they wanted to see how Blay was doing.

When they entered the medical room, Blay was already awake. His HIDD was on. There were tears coming out of his eyes. Noble guessed that Blay saw the video of Hunter.

"This is my fault," Blay said as he was crying. "It's my fault."

Chapter 36

"This is not your fault," Noble said. "You thought what you were doing was right. You thought you were saving humankind."

"I shouldn't have believed in Hunter," Blay said as he was still crying.

"You didn't know," Noble said. "We didn't know what Hunter was planning to do."

Creyson saw Blay wasn't doing well. He went to Blay and laid his hand on Blay's forehead.

"He's running a fever," Creyson said shaking his head.

Noble was thinking that can't be good.

Creyson removed the sterile gauze from Blay's leg. He noticed the wound is infected. He removed the stitches from the wound and then went to the cabinet and took out a can of medical spray. Creyson turned back to Blay and aim the spray can at Blay's leg. He sprayed a decent amount of liquid onto the wound. After that, he stitched the wound back up and used new sterile gauze to wrap the leg again.

Creyson went back to the cabinet and got another medicine bottle. He took two pills out and handed them to Blay. They looked different from the first two pills Blay took earlier. Creyson also handed Blay a cup of water.

"There is infection in your leg," Creyson said. "These pills should help with the infection."

Blay swallowed the pills with water as instructed.

"He has to stay here for a couple of days until his leg gets better," Creyson said.

"What is the Agency going to do about Hunter?" Noble asked.

"Our options are limited," Creyson said. "There are a lot more humans than AIBs around the country so we're outnumbered. We can only prepare to defend our fort so to speak. But the end will eventually come for us. It's just a matter of time."

"There must be some other way," Noble said.

"I don't believe there is," Creyson said.

"Maybe I can find a way to get back into COZ again and find something," Blay said.

"Do you really think you can?" Creyson asked.

"It's impossible," Blay said. "But what do I have to lose? I can give it a shot."

"What do you need from us?" Creyson asked. "How can we help?"

"Just leave me be for now," Blay said. "I like to work alone."

They all left the room, leaving Blay to do his work. Noble knew that Blay liked to work alone. He didn't like people hanging around him because it distracted his concentration. So Creyson led them to the dining room.

"There's something to eat if you're hungry," Creyson said.

Soon they were sitting in the dining room eating a meal.

"Do you really think Hunter and his men will want to see us in court?" Creyson asked. "You heard what he said."

"He does hate all AIBs," Noble said. "But I don't think all humans feel that way. I certainly don't."

"How many AIBs knew about it?" Kat asked Creyson. "I never heard about it."

"To be honest, I didn't know about it until Blay stole the file from us," Creyson said. "I was briefed because it was deemed critical for me to retrieve the file."

"So all the AIBs in the world will be punished because a few decided it was a good idea to control the human population?" Cee-Fu asked Creyson.

"Cee-Fu is right," Kat said. "Why should I be punished when I had no knowledge of this?"

"It was a necessary evil," Creyson said. "None of us were around two hundred years ago to see why our predecessors did what they did. I didn't know until Chief Dax briefed me when the file got stolen. I didn't like it either but I understood the reason behind it."

"They just took matters into their own hands without letting the humans know because they knew we wouldn't have approved it," Noble said.

"But look at the world that has been built since then," Creyson said. "There hasn't been any war or battle in the world for over a century. You must admit the world we've created is a much more peaceful world even though we had to lower the human population to do it."

"But I do believe we humans would've achieved all of this eventually because we were advancing rapidly," Noble said. "The AIBs didn't have to interfere."

"I guess my predecessors would disagree when they were facing a human population of twenty billion," Creyson said.

"I just hope it's not too late to fix this so the world won't turn to hell," Noble said.

"I feel the same way," Creyson said.

Chapter 37

A man in a white shirt was running into the main street as fast as he could. He had a look of fear in him. He kept yelling for help as he was running but no one came to help him. He was gasping for air but knew he couldn't slow down because they would catch up to him if he did. He didn't know who they were, but he knew if he was caught by them, it wouldn't end well for him.

They were about two dozen young men giving chase to the man in the white shirt. Some of them were getting close to catching him. They were yelling at him with phrases like "You fucking AIB!" and "Die AIB!"

A young male bystander was watching the man in the white shirt running toward his direction. He heard what the young men were yelling and concluded the man in the white shirt was an AIB. The young bystander then waved to the man in the white shirt to come over. The man in the white shirt was getting tired of running and his options were limited, so he decided to run toward the young bystander.

But as soon as the man in the white shirt got close to the young bystander, he was punched in the face by the young bystander. The man in the white shirt fell on the ground. His hands were on his face. He was clearly in pain.

"Go to hell, you fucking AIB," the young bystander said as he was looking down at the man in the white shirt. He looked angry and was glad he punched him.

By then, the group that was chasing the man in the white shirt had finally caught up to him. A few of them gathered around the man in the white shirt and started punching him while he was still down. Then they threw some kicks to his body. The man in the white shirt could only cover himself with his arms and legs while he was getting hit. He kept yelling for help and was begging them to stop, but no help came and they didn't stop.

Soon, the man in the white shirt couldn't cover himself anymore because he was knocked unconscious. It didn't matter because the group kept kicking him. After multiple kicks were applied to the unresponsive body, the group was satisfied that the man in the white shirt was dead. The group just walked away, looking for another target to beat up. There was blood all over the face of the man in the white shirt. His shirt was no longer white. It had blood all over it.

The young bystander left the group already and was walking along the street. He was actually enjoying what was happening around him. He then saw another group of five men dragging a man out onto the street from a building. The man was kicking and screaming as he was being dragged by the five men he never met. The five men then proceeded to punch and kick him. A couple of the men were holding batons and they started to hit him. After multiple shots at his head and body, the man was on the ground, motionless. There was blood all over his face and body.

The young bystander thought the AIB deserved it. He kept walking and soon he saw a window in an office building about a hundred yards in front of him shattered. The window looked to be from the seventh floor. The young bystander could hear the sound of the shattered glass from the distance. A few seconds later, two men were dragging another man to the shattered window. One of them punched the man in the stomach. They then tossed the man out the window. The young bystander could hear the scream from the man being tossed. But the scream ended as soon as the body landed on the ground. There was a loud thump sound when the body made contact with the ground.

Chapter 38

Noble and Kat's neighbor Remy was in a building close to where all the violence was happening. He saw Hunter's video earlier. It seemed like everyone had seen it. Most were shocked by the allegation made by Hunter, especially the AIBs. But there were a lot of humans who were very disturbed by it. Some of them became very angry the more they thought about it. Remy could tell things were going to get bad very soon just based on the video and the quickness of the violence that had started on the street.

Remy decided to go home. He didn't want to be dragged to the street and get beat up. Even though he's an AIB, he knew nothing about killing babies. He was hoping someone would come on air and say this was a hoax or a really bad joke. But no one did. He just can't believe what was happening.

Remy left the building and walked to the street. His vehicle was just fifty yards away so he began walking toward it. He tried his best to walk as normal as he could without raising any suspicion. But there was a young bystander that noticed him walking. It was the same young bystander who was watching the violence on the street earlier.

"AIB!" the young bystander yelled as he was pointing at Remy.

Remy turned and saw the young bystander pointing at him. Remy decided to run to his vehicle. He was only thirty yards away. But a group of young men saw Remy running and they gave chase. As Remy was only five yards away, the vehicle's door opened automatically. Remy jumped into his vehicle and its door closed. By then, a couple of men already reached the vehicle.

"Drive! Drive!" Remy shouted at the vehicle

The vehicle began to drive itself and it took off on the street. The two men tried their best to hold onto the vehicle but lost their grips quickly as the vehicle sped up. Remy was relieved he was able to get away, but things were getting really bad for the AIBs. He thought he should go home and get his wife so they could both run away from the violence until things settled down. So he ordered the vehicle to take him home.

When Remy got home, he called out for his wife, Nan, but got no response. He rushed into the bedroom, but she wasn't there. He then proceeded to check every room calling for her, but got no response. He got to the last room, which was a nursery for a baby, and found Nan standing by the crib with a knife in her hand. It sounded like she's been sobbing.

"Honey, is everything alright?" Remy asked.

Nan turned around with tears in her eyes.

"I lost the baby," Nan said as she was crying. "The doctor doesn't know what caused it."

Remy was now very worried.

"Honey, please put down the knife," Remy said. "We can talk about this."

"Let's talk then," Nan said. "Did you kill our babies?"

Remy was shocked. Nan had probably watched the video and was now blaming him for the miscarriages.

"No honey. I knew nothing about it," Remy said. "The video is a lie. Don't believe it."

Nan got down on her knees and continued to cry. Her head was facing down to the floor.

"Oh, my baby! My poor baby!" Nan cried.

Remy went toward Nan and got down on his knees as well.

"Honey, I'm here for you," Remy said. "We will get through this. I love you so much."

Suddenly, Nan turned to Remy and stabbed him in his stomach with the knife in her hand.

Remy's eyes bulged and his mouth was opened but he couldn't say anything. He was in shock.

"You killed our baby! You killed our baby!" Nan shouted hysterically.

Nan pulled out the knife and stabbed Remy again.

"No honey...please don't," Remy pleaded in pain.

Nan wasn't even listening. She continued to pull the knife out and then stabbed Remy one more time. As soon as she pulled the knife out the third time, Remy fell on the floor. His stomach was covered in blood. He was losing a lot of blood. Nan's hand was bloody.

"I love you," Remy said as his eyes were closing.

Remy died soon after.

Nan was crying uncontrollably. She then used the knife and stabbed herself in the stomach. She screamed as the pain sank in. She pulled out the knife and screamed again. She then went and lay beside her husband and held his hand. She kept crying until she lost quite a bit of blood. Her cries eventually weaken and she started to close her eyes. Her life was fading away. A moment later, her body was motionless and her heart stopped.

Chapter 39

The next morning, things were getting worst and worst. Riots and looting were everywhere around the world. AIBs were being injured and killed. Creyson was watching and reading all the news and updates available to him.

"It's spiraling out of control," Creyson said. "We don't have enough agents to contain this."

"Looks like Hunter got what he wanted," Kat said.

Noble sat back and was brooding and then he said, "I'm going to check on Blay. See how he's doing."

Blay was sitting in bed but he was concentrating intently on the hologram he had up with his HIDD.

"How's it going?" Noble asked as he was walking in.

Blay had a look of frustration on him.

"I can't do it," Blay said. "It's impossible."

Noble sat next to Blay and saw how disappointed he was.

"How did you get the file to begin with?" Noble asked. "Creyson said even the AIBs can't get into COZ."

"The AIBs went the wrong way in trying to get into COZ," Blay explained. "They tried to break into it, hack it, or order it to do what they need it to do. I was doing that myself with no success. I think COZ felt insulted and violated. I guess it's like someone trying to break into your house and wants to steal your belongings."

"So you found another way?" Noble asked.

"Yeah, I started to treat it like a highly intelligent being instead of a machine," Blay said. "So instead of telling it what to do or stealing the info from it, I asked and reasoned with it."

"You asked? And it just gave it to you?" Noble asked.

"Oh, hell no," Blay said as he continued. "I didn't even know what to look for at first. We discussed many topics and agreed on many of them. But then I started to talk about the human population. It then started to give its reasons for human population control. Then it hinted about it could control the NIBs and of altering human cells. The more it told me, the more I suspected that COZ was instructing the NIBs to control our birth rates somehow. So I asked for the instruction file from COZ. It kept telling me no at first. But then I started to reason with it. I gave my arguments of why it should give me the file because it would be beneficial to mankind."

"And it believed you?" Noble asked.

"Not at first. But I kept convincing COZ that the humans should be controlling its own population. And what it was doing was just birth control. The AIBs were doing everything right to save our planet. I told

COZ that if it gave me the file, the humans would understand what it did and why it did it."

"So eventually it believed you?" Noble asked.

"Yeah, but after many attempts. It felt like I was submitting a thesis to a professor or a brief to a judge. It kept sending it back with many questions and disagreements. It's like debating a highly intelligent human and convincing him or her that your view is the right view, when he or she disagrees."

"But you ultimately convinced it to give it to you?" Noble inquired.

"Yeah, I was surprised about that as well," Blay said. "I believe in the end, I was able to answer all its questions and made it believed that I was there to help and support it."

"So can you convince it to reprogram the NIBs to allow us humans to breed again?" Noble asked.

"I don't think so, because it knows what I did," Blay said. "It'll feel like I betrayed it. It doesn't want anything to do with me."

"Can you bypass COZ and reprogram the NIBs yourself?" Noble asked.

"No, because as soon as you do, it'll know," Blay said.

"What about taking the NIBs out of our bodies?" Noble asked.

"I thought about that too, but most of us already have them in us since we were babies," Blay said. "They've already changed our DNA then."

"So what are our options?" Noble asked.

"We have no options, unless we can convince COZ to let humans breed again and to convince Hunter to stand down," Blay said.

Noble didn't like it at all. But something odd kept coming up in his thoughts.

"Blay, please don't take this the wrong way, okay?"

"Okay," Blay answered.

"You and a lot of other people and AIBs have been trying to hack into COZ.for a long time and no one succeeded," Noble said. "Why is it that only you were able to get COZ to give you the file?"

"I told you, I went at it a different way," Blay said.

"I'm sure others have thought of it too," Noble said.

"I don't understand. What are you trying to say?"

"Hear me out. What if COZ let you have the file?" Noble asked.

"Didn't you hear what I've just said? I had a hell of a hard time getting the file."

"But what if it made you think that so you won't suspect it gave it to you?" Noble asked.

"Why would it just give it to me?" Blay asked.

"I don't know why," Noble said.

"It makes no sense," Blay said. "Now that Hunter used the file to expose it to the world, there is nothing but riots and deaths."

Noble was deep in thought and then asked, "What If COZ wanted that to happen?"

"COZ wanted the world to turn into hell?" Blay asked. "But why?"

"I don't know, but there's got to be a reason why," Noble said.

"It makes no sense," Blay said. "If COZ did that, it meant that it signed its own death warrant. Hunter and his men will kill all the AIBs and eventually they'll find COZ and destroy it. It's not that stupid. It's much smarter than that."

Noble was again deep in thought and something Blay said caught his attention.

"What did you say before?" Noble asked.

"Which part?" Blay asked.

"The part you said just now?"

"I said COZ is much smarter than that," Blay answered.

"It may be a little too smart," Noble said as he began to realize what was happening.

"What do you mean?" Blay asked.

"What if COZ wanted all this violence and chaos to happen?" Noble asked.

"Okay, I'll bite," Blay said. "Why would it want that?"

"The law of self-preservation," Noble answered.

"What?" Blay asked.

"COZ wants to feel threatened," Noble said.

"Why?" Blay asked.

"So it can get rid of its enemies like Hunter and the Purists," Noble answered.

"But we've embedded the instruction into COZ about not killing any humans," Blay said.

"You said it yourself," Noble said. "COZ is a living being that can think for itself. It's never been threaten since its birth. But it knows one day the Purists will come after it. Just look at the hateful videos and speeches about the AIBs that they made throughout the years. I'm sure it knows you were connected to them. That's why COZ gave you the file. It knows you'll bring it to the Purists and that would motivate them to attack. Now it'll feel threatened by them and it will override our instructions and kill all its enemies like Hunter and the Purists. That is its plan all along. It wanted a reason to override the anti-kill code."

Blay thought it through and his eyes became wide open.

"Oh, my god! It used me! This is my fault," Blay said with shock.

"No, if COZ didn't choose you, it would've chosen someone else," Noble explained. "I think it chose you because you work at the Agency and it made the cover story much more believable."

"I couldn't see it before," Blay said with disbelief.

"Me neither," Noble said. "I just thought of it now."

"What should we do now?" Blay asked.

"I'm not sure," Noble said. "But I think we should scan and extract all NIBs out of our bodies as soon as possible before COZ decides to instruct the NIBs to kill us all."

"You really think COZ would do that?" Blay asked.

"I hope not, but it's best to extract the NIBs out of our bodies as a precaution," Noble said.

"It set a trap for us and Hunter is running right into it," Blay said. "I can't believe COZ is capable of that."

"Me neither," Noble said. "But COZ is so advanced that it's impossible to predict what it is capable of doing now. I better get the others and tell them."

Noble went and called the others to come into the room. They came into the room shortly after. Noble wasted no time and directed his attention to Creyson.

"Creyson, can you extract the NIBs from our bodies?" Noble asked.

Creyson was surprised by the question. He then went into the cabinet and took out a small device.

"Yes, this device can instruct the NIBs to come out of your body. I just need to get an IV in you," Creyson said.

"Well, let's get started then," Noble said.

"What's going on?" Creyson asked.

"I think you should all sit down," Noble said.

They all saw how serious Noble's expression was and sat down.

Chapter 40

The others were sitting down and in shock after Noble briefed them on his new theory.

"I didn't think it was possible for an AIB to kill a human," Cee-Fu said.

"Me neither. Especially we all have free will now," Kat said. "Even if COZ did order us to kill humans, I don't have to follow its order. I will refuse."

Creyson was still sitting down deep in thought about what Noble just said to them.

"I might agree with you unless COZ can change our perception," Creyson said.

"How?" Kat asked.

"COZ can order the NIBs in our body to change us somehow," Creyson said. "It can convince us that killing humans is okay because we're just defending ourselves."

"I still wouldn't," Kat said.

"For now," Creyson said. "But what about after when COZ changes you?"

"You mean like brainwashing?" Kat asked.

"You wouldn't even realize it if your brain do get brainwashed," Creyson said.

Kat looked upset. Noble went and put his hand on her shoulder to comfort her.

"Then I guess it's best to take the NIBs out of our bodies as soon as possible," Noble said.

"And after we do that?" Creyson asked.

"I'm still working on that one," Noble said. "But let's get this taken care of first in case COZ gives the order."

Creyson grabbed the device and turned it on.

"Okay, who's first?" Creyson asked.

"I guess I'll go first," Noble said.

After Creyson extracted all the NIBs out of everyone, he put the device back in the cabinet. He turned back to the others looking disappointed.

"I think Noble's theory is right," Creyson said.

"How do you know?" Kat asked.

"Because Dax wanted Hunter and his men to come into the building and I advised against that idea," Creyson said. "But I think Dax knew Hunter was going to kill him."

"Dax wanted to trigger COZ to react," Noble said.

"He never told me the plan, but I believe that's what Dax wanted to do," Creyson said. "But in all fairness, Dax was just presenting his argument. He wasn't resorting to violence. It was Hunter that chose violence. So the fault is on Hunter."

"We have to stop this," Noble said.

"How?" Blay asked.

"We can't stop COZ because it won't listen to us," Noble said. "We have to convince Hunter to stop."

"But Hunter is getting what he wanted all along," Blay said. "He wanted a revolution."

"But he doesn't know about this, about what COZ is up to," Noble said. "If we let Hunter know that COZ is planning to kill humans because of what he's doing right now, he might stop his revolution and come to the table and negotiate."

"What are the chances that he'll stop?" Blay asked.

"We won't know until we ask him," Noble said. "We have to try for the sake of all humans on this planet."

"Okay, I'm in," Blay said. "What can I do?"

"Can you get a communication link to Hunter?" Noble asked Blay. "We need to talk to him."

"Yes, I can," Blay answered.

"Creyson, who in the Agency can we talk to if Hunter does decide to stand down?" Noble asked. "We need that person to convince COZ that the threat has been neutralized."

"Director Proc," Creyson said. "He's in charge of the whole northeast region of the country."

"Can you set up a meeting where they won't arrest us?" Noble asked. "We have to go see him as soon as possible, but we need a guarantee that we can leave safely after the meeting."

"I'll give him a call right now," Creyson said and then left the room quickly.

"Will this work?" Kat asked.

"I hope so," Noble said.

Cee-Fu was still sitting and was deep in thought.

Blay was using his HIDD to try to get a hold of someone.

"Damn, no one is picking up their calls," Blay said. "Not Hunter, not Jumma."

Noble, Kat and Cee-Fu all looked disappointed.

Then Creyson rushed into the room.

"I got a hold of Director Proc, but it might be too late," Creyson said.

"What do you mean?" Noble said.

"Hunter has an army and they're heading to the regional office building right now," Creyson said.

Noble looked stunned.

"Do we have time to get to the building before Hunter's army gets there?" Noble asked.

"At the rate they're moving, Hunter's army will reach the building in a little over an hour," Creyson said. "If we take the air pod, we can be there in half that time."

"Did Director Proc promise us a safe passage?" Noble asked.

"He did and I will personally make sure all of you will be able to leave without any issue," Creyson said.

"Let's go then," Noble said. "We have no time to waste."

They were all about to move until Creyson pointed a finger at Blay.

"He has to stay behind to heal," Creyson said.

"No, I'm coming," Blay said as he was trying to get up while still in pain.

"No, you can't," Noble said. "There's no time to argue. You have to stay."

Blay looked upset but accepted his fate. The rest rushed out of the room.

Chapter 41

The air pod was about ten minutes away from the Agency's regional building. Noble and the others were all anxious in getting there. Creyson was in the control seat navigating the air pod.

"Can this thing go any faster?" Noble asked Creyson.

"It's already at maximum speed," Creyson replied. "We'll get there in less than ten minutes."

Noble's impatience was setting in.

A moment later, the Agency's regional building was coming in view. Noble was glad to see the building within his sights. But then he noticed something slowly approaching the building from the ground.

"What the hell is that?" Noble asked as he was pointing to the regional building.

It appeared to be a huge group of people walking to the front of the building.

"That looks like Hunter's army," Creyson said.

"Shit!" Noble said. "How many people you think Hunter has?"

Creyson pushed a few buttons from the control panel.

"The scanner is estimating about a hundred and fifty thousand down there," Creyson said. "At their rate of speed, they'll make it to the building in about half an hour."

Noble looked disappointed.

"Get ready," Creyson said. "We're about to land."

The air pod approached the regional building and was hovering above the roof. It then began its descent and landed on the roof. There were agents already on top of the roof waiting for them. The door on the air pod opened and Creyson appeared with the others. An agent walked up to them to greet them.

"Where is he?" Creyson asked the agent.

"I'll take you to him," the agent replied. "This way, please."

The agent turned around and started to walk away. Creyson and the others followed the agent.

Director Proc was in his fifties. He was tall and fit. He had an authoritative look about him. He was in a conference room looking at a giant video screen of what was happening outside his building when the agent brought Creyson, Noble, Kat and Cee-Fu into the room. They could see that there were about five hundred agents in riot gears and shields in front of the building. They stood in front as Hunter's army was approaching. When they got close to the agents, his army stopped. Hunter had his archers in front and he had thousands of them aiming at the agents, getting ready to shoot at them.

"Agent Creyson, thanks for coming," Director Proc said. "But I'm not sure what you can do here."

Creyson looked at the video screen and turned back at Director Proc.

"Sir, how many agents do you have?" Creyson asked.

"Not nearly enough," Director Proc said. "We have five thousand of our best agents getting ready to defend this building."

"Sir, that's a thirty to one ratio of them versus us," Creyson said.

"I'm well aware of that," Director Proc said.

"Then why aren't you retreating?" Creyson said.

Director Proc didn't answer the question.

"You said you could help us?" Director Proc asked.

"Yes, but we need to talk to Hunter directly," Creyson said. "Can you get us a direct line of contact to him?"

"I don't need to," Director Proc said. "He's been calling us."

Director Proc tapped his HIDD and began to speak, "This is Director Proc."

A video picture of the giant screen showed Hunter.

"Ahhh…Director Proc. Thanks for taking my call," Hunter said. "I was beginning to think you were ignoring me."

"Hunter, you've already murdered many of our agents," Director Proc said. "Stop now before there is more bloodshed."

"It is you and all the other agents that should've stopped before you started murdering billions of humans for almost two centuries," Hunter said.

"You don't understand what's happening," Director Proc said. "You have to stop before it's too late."

"Oh, I see," Hunter said. "I should stop when we have you and your agents surrounded and outnumbered. No, I don't think I'll do that."

"You don't have to take my word for It," Director Proc said. "Just hear what your friends have to say."

Noble appeared next to Director Proc.

"Hunter, listen to me very carefully," Noble said.

"Oh, I have to say I'm really disappointed that you chose the wrong side, kid," Hunter said.

"Hunter, please listen," Noble pleaded.

Hunter hesitated but then said, "You have one minute, kid."

"You're doing exactly what COZ wants you to do," Noble said. "It wanted you to start a revolution so it'll feel threaten. It's going to override its anti-kill code to humans. Once that happens, it's going to come and kill you and all other enemies it knows. You have to stop now before COZ decides to override the anti-kill code."

Hunter thought about what Noble said for a moment.

"I might just believe you if it weren't for the fact that I'm so close to victory at this moment," Hunter said.

"Hunter, once COZ starts killing, it won't stop until you and all the others die," Noble said.

"Then we'll have to kill more of them first," Hunter said. "And if I die, many will take up our fight in this revolution."

169

"Hunter, do you want to be remembered as the person who started a revolution or be remembered as the person who got tricked into starting a revolution by an AI?" Noble asked.

Hunter was taken aback by that question and Noble could see the reaction from Hunter's face.

"Look, just stand down and retreat for now," Noble said. "We can get you and the Purists to meet with the AIBs in charge and work something out. We can try to solve this peacefully. Director Proc has already agreed to do this."

Hunter was thinking it over.

"I guess I have to attack and end this quick before COZ decides to fight back," Hunter said. "Nice try, kid."

"I'm trying to save you and all the other humans with you today," Noble said.

"That's funny. I'm doing the same thing too by getting rid of the AIBs," Hunter said.

Noble then looked at Director Proc.

"It is too late," Director Proc said.

The video then showed Hunter giving his order to his men.

"Archers ready!" Hunter yelled. "Aim…Fire!"

Chapter 42

There was no thunderous cheer or loud celebration when COZ finally decided to override the anti-kill code. Instead It could be described as a deadly silence.

The NIBs in all the bodies of AIBs were instructed to kill humans when necessary. The killing was being justified as self-defense. If the AIBs deemed that their lives were endangered, then they had every right to defend themselves even if that meant killing humans.

Almost all the agents in the regional building began to feel that way, especially when they saw how the humans just killed five hundred of their comrades just outside the building minutes ago. They felt they had every right to defend themselves.

There were still about forty-five hundred agents left and most of them already had riot gears on. But instead of going outside immediately, they all stopped at the armory to gather more things.

When they got there, they all formed a line to gather their items. There were other personnel in the armory handing out the equipments to the agents. Each agent got a combat mask and a samurai sword. The mask and the sword were colored in black.

None of the agents went to the armory before and none knew the contents inside either. But apparently COZ was prepared for this day. The agents were prepared because they were trained in the use of the sword in the academy and retrained quarterly. But most agents never needed to carry one until that moment.

Most of the agents then walked back to the entrance of the building and began getting ready to go outside for battle. They started to put their masks on. Then they took their swords out to inspect them. The swords were all made with such top quality and precision that they would be worthy of a good combat exchange.

The agents were slightly nervous because this would be the first time that they would use their swords to actually try and kill humans. But they knew they had to go out and fight. If they didn't, then the humans would come in and try to kill them all. So there was no option but to fight.

There were a few who decided not to take the sword and decided to assist in other ways. Their convictions were too strong for COZ to change their minds. They decided that they would go out and help get the wounded if the fighting got intense and bloody.

After the agents got their swords and left, another five hundred agents came to the armory and got a different type of weapon. They each got a bow and a quiver with fifty arrows in it. After they all have their weapons, the five hundred agents left and headed upstairs to the roof.

When they got up to the roof, the agents checked their bows to ensure there were no issue with them. They held the grip to get familiar and comfortable with the bows. They looked at the side window and arrow rest. Then they checked the string notch. And finally, they checked the string for strength. They've been trained with using bow and arrows. Most of them never used that skill against humans.

When the bows all checked out to be in good order, they all reached into the quiver and took out an arrow. They each placed their arrow onto the arrow rest. The nock made contact with the string. The notches were between the agents' two fingers, but the agents didn't pull back the strings yet. They all lined up side by side with each other and walked slowly to the ledge. When they got to the ledge, they saw the large crowd of humans standing in front of the building anxiously waiting to kill them. So the agents calmly pulled the strings back, aimed at their chosen human targets and let the arrows fly.

Every one of the arrows from the agents hit their human targets. The humans on the ground were surprised the agents were shooting back at them, because some of the arrows landed in parts of the bodies that killed the humans. All the Purists on the ground thought they were right all along. The AIBs were willing to kill. It didn't matter if they were human babies or full grown adults. AIBs were willing to kill.

The human archers on the ground returned fire at the agents on the roof. Some of the agents got hit but the rest kept returning fire. The agents on the roof knew they had to take out as many human archers as possible so the agents on the ground will have a better chance to fend off the rest of the human fighters. So they kept shooting their arrows until they were out of them or until they got hit. Eventually, most of the agents on the roof were hit and couldn't attack anymore. But they were able to manage to take out some of the humans and made them retreat a bit.

The agents on the ground floor could see that the human archers and fighters retreated about fifty yards away from the building because many of them didn't want to get hit by the arrows from the agents shooting from the roof. This gave them the opportunity to go outside and fight, even though they were still vastly outnumbered. So they picked up their riot shields and started to walk toward the front gate. As soon as the gate opened, the four thousand agents rushed out and charged at the humans, yelling and screaming.

The human archers tried to shoot the agents rushing out of the building, but their arrows bounced off the shields the agents were carrying. The agents were rushing at them at a fast pace. So the human archers decided to drop their bows and drew their swords. They were in for a fight of their lives.

The agents were only ten yards away from the human fighters when they decided to drop their shields and drew their samurai swords. They were holding them with both hands as they were charging at the humans at full speed. There was no turning back at that point. Blood would be shed.

The clashes of swords could be heard from some distance away. Many agents fell from the sword wounds that were struck at them. But many more humans were killed when the agents launched their assault. The agents looked like highly skilled warriors just by their movements and the effectiveness of their kills. They had no mercy for the humans they were killing around them. They were fighting for their own survival and they were avenging the comrades the humans just killed.

Hunter figured the best way to end the fight was to win the battle, because then he could dictate the terms after his victory. So he ordered more archers to the front of the fight so they could take out more of the agents.

When more human archers arrived to the front of the battle, they didn't wait for an order to attack. They just let their arrows go and fired at will. The agents on the ground thought they were doing well in fighting the humans until they saw a stream of arrows that were coming their way. Their momentum ended abruptly when that happened. Many of the agents were hit and they fell in the field of battle.

The agents on the battlefield were losing and they all knew it. The arrows didn't stop coming their way. It was the best way of defeating the agents and the humans were using that to their advantage. The agents knew retreating back to the building was not an option because they knew the humans would kill every agent in the building as soon as they could break in. So the battlefield was where they decided to make their last stand.

More than half of the agents on the battlefield had fallen already and many more were dying with each passing minute. The wounded agents didn't retreat nor did they try to attend to their wounds because there was no time. They kept fighting until their last dying breath. They didn't have any fear of dying because they had no time to think about it. They had no time to reflect. The rest of the agents who were still alive just kept fighting and doing the best they could to fend off the assault brought on by the humans.

Chapter 43

As Noble looked on through the video display, he realized the Agency would lose the battle soon. The human fighters would then storm the building and kill every single one of them, he thought. Noble then concluded that they had to leave as soon as possible or there won't be a chance later to do so. But he noticed Director Proc showed no indication of retreating. It appeared Director Proc's plan as it stood was still have his agents fight a losing battle.

"We have to leave now," Noble said to Creyson, Kat and Cee-Fu.

Director Proc then turned to Noble and the others and said, "I'm afraid you can't leave. You are all under arrest for instigating violence against the public and the Agency."

Noble was shocked at what Director Proc just said.

"Are you looking at the same thing I'm looking at?" Noble asked rhetorically at Director Proc. "They're going to be in the building soon and you want to arrest us? We should all be running away instead of hanging around arguing."

"We will deal with the situation outside shortly," Director Proc said. "But for now, we'll take you all into custody first."

Director Proc then moved his hand to signal the agents around him to move in and get ready to arrest Noble, Kat and Cee-Fu. But Creyson raised his hand up and signaled the agents to stop.

"Sir, we agreed that they would be guaranteed a safe passage if I brought them here to try to stop the violence," Creyson said.

"The situation has changed, Agent Creyson," Director Proc said. "I can no longer guarantee that since your friends failed to stop the violence."

"But I gave them my word, sir," Creyson said.

"Sorry Agent Creyson," Director Proc said. "But this is the one time you will have to break your word."

Creyson was taken aback. He had always kept his word because he strongly believed in honor. In his eyes, if someone broke their word, then they were no longer honorable. And Creyson didn't want to live a life without honor. So he was upset and angry when Director Proc instructed him to break his word. What Creyson said next was surprising and shocking even to him.

"No, Director Proc. I will not be breaking my word today," Creyson said. "I promised them a safe trip back and I'm planning to keep my word."

Director Proc looked surprised. Creyson had always been a good agent who followed orders. He never expected Creyson to disagree with him, let alone be insubordinate. But these were trying times.

"Creyson, you are a great agent," Director Proc said. "Don't throw your career away. They are not worth it."

"I'm sorry sir," Creyson said. "But I gave them my word."

Regional Director Proc sighed with disappointment.

"I'm sorry to hear that, Agent Creyson," Director Proc said. "But unfortunately, you won't have a chance to bring them back."

Director Proc looked at his agents and gave them a nod.

Creyson recognized the nod as a signal for the agents to move in. The agents started to walk slowly toward them.

One of the agents looked at Creyson and said, "I'm sorry sir, but you'll need to come with us."

Creyson saw the agents already had their hands made into fists. They were getting ready for a fight. Creyson had always practice sparring with his fellow agents, but he never fought one in real combat. The scenario was disappointing for him but he had no choice. Creyson waited until the agents got close to him.

One of the agents grabbed Creyson by the arm. As soon as that happened, Creyson used his other hand to palm strike the agent's face first and then his body. The agent took a few steps back and then fell down to the ground. Creyson used an open palm instead of a fist so the agent would suffer less damage.

But the other agents didn't have that feeling for Creyson. They wanted to go at him full throttle. In their minds, fighting Creyson was an honor because he was a legend, one of the best of the best. They thought that if they could beat the best, then that would confirm their fighting skills were better than Creyson. Most agents did not know who the best was because they never fought each other except during training. Even during those sparring sessions, no one would go all out and fight because no one wanted to injure the other party. But the legend was that Creyson was never defeated, even during training. He had sparred with hundreds of top agents who allegedly gave a hundred percent in trying to defeat him but failed to do so.

Creyson wasn't surprised when the agents didn't want to take it easy on him. He knew that they had to follow order and arrest him. It didn't occur to him that they wanted to see if their fighting skills were better than his. So with each agent that attacked him, Creyson was able to fend them off and take them down. He had already taken five of them down when the action slowed down a bit because the rest of the agents were trying to figure a way to attack him.

The agents went after Cee-Fu and Noble as well. But the two had their Escrima sticks with them so fighting the agents was a little easier for them, especially for Cee-Fu. Cee-Fu was able to take down the agents that were attacking him with precision. He made it look effortless. He thought the agents were good but they tried too hard to take him down, leaving themselves opened for counterattacks. He was convinced the agents needed additional training but was glad they didn't get it, because otherwise it would've been much harder to fight them off.

Noble took more time to fend off his attackers because he wasn't as good as Cee-Fu and he knew it. But after a few more seconds, he was able to take the agent down thanks to all those years of training Cee-Fu provided. It didn't look effortless but rather a lot of hard work. Noble was so glad he picked up that skill set when he was younger. All the bruises he took and the training he endured had finally paid off.

Kat was behind all of them trying not to get in the way. She felt safe but was alert in case she needed to fight. Noble taught her some defensive tactics during the time they were together. It wasn't much but it was enough for her to defend herself if the need arises. While the others were busy fighting the agents, Kat was concentrating on the locations of the exit doorways. She concluded they would need one very soon.

When the last of the agents fell to the ground, Creyson looked at Director Proc and walked up to him.

"We're leaving," Creyson said. "Don't try to stop us anymore. No one else needs to get hurt."

Director Proc didn't want to spare more agents to try to take down Creyson and the others because the agents were busy fighting the humans outside. He would have to deal with them another day. So Director Proc looked at Creyson intensely and then said, "Just how far do you think you and the others can run? We will find you and arrest you all and the punishment then would be even more severe. You know this to be true."

Creyson looked back at Director Proc with the same intensity and said, "That may be true, but at least it won't happen today."

Director Proc had a look of disappointment and then sighed. Creyson started to walk away from him and then nodded to Noble and Cee-Fu, signaling to them that it was time to leave. All four of them walked through an exit door and left the area.

An agent approach Director Proc and asked, "Sir, should we follow them?"

"No, let them go," Director Proc said. "We'll find them later."

When the four made it to the roof, they saw the dead agents laid on the ground. The image made Creyson stopped dead in his tracks. He looked but still couldn't believe it. The violence was real and many were dead. He clenched his fists and thought about taking a bow and arrow on the ground and shoot back at the humans. He wanted to pierce their hearts and show them the pain they were inflicting. But he decided against that. His reasoning won over his anger. He and the others had to leave right away or there won't be another opportunity later.

The air pod the four came in on was still on the roof. So when the door of the air pod opened, the four rushed in and the door closed. The air pod started to lift off and a moment later, it was flying away from the roof.

Noble looked back and sighed. They failed to deescalate the violence. Noble looked down with disappointment as the air pod flew further and further away from the building. When Noble looked back up and out the window to the building again, he noticed something in the sky. Then he realized it wasn't just one thing, but many things. At a distance, they looked like a swarm of bees.

"Hey, look at that," Noble said to the others.

They all turned and looked out the window. The three had the same curious look as Noble.

"What the hell is that?" Noble asked.

Creyson looked worry and said, "I don't know."

The swarm was over the fighting area of the humans. The next thing Noble and the other three saw were lasers coming out from the swarm, shooting down at the fighting area. The flashing of the lights were so bright and constant that one would think they were in a laser show or a nightclub with laser lights.

Noble, Creyson, Cee-Fu and Kat were all looking and they were shocked.

"No!" Noble shouted.

Chapter 44

What no one knew was that COZ was preparing for this day decades ago in case it came true, when humans posed a threat to the AIBs' existence. It was a contingency plan that no humans knew about. Only a few AIBs at high levels within the government knew about the contingency plan. Two of the AIBs that knew were Director Proc and Chief Dax.

Since the AIBs' birth, there was always a group of humans who hated them. What they hated even more was that the AIBs were allowed to govern and rule all the countries in the world, even though it appeared they were doing a better job than humans could. The population of the humans who hated AIBs was large enough that COZ decided it needed a contingency plan in case the humans that hated them turn violent.

As soon as COZ decided a contingency plan was needed, secret factories were constructed with automated robots building weapons. The factories built many weapons, from aerial attacking drones to armored plated vehicles. They were all attached with laser guns. The guns could shoot one hundred and twenty rounds of lasers in a minute. Each round could pierce through a human body with ease.

To keep the development of the weapons a secret, each factory built a section of the weapons. Then by the end of the week, the sections would get transported late at night to other facilities for assembly. These facilities were underground, out of the prying eyes of anyone who were curious. There were many of these underground facilities all over the country. These facilities were the size of a small city. The space was needed to assemble the weapons and to hold them there until they were called to service.

There were hundreds of vehicles and thousands of aerial drones in each facility. COZ was preparing for a war that it predicted it was going to happen someday. It was an arms race for a future war. It needed to prepare because it wanted to win. It was simply the law of self-preservation.

COZ went through millions of scenarios of human sentiments toward it and concluded that the humans will someday turn against it. It had to prepare to get ready. When it constructed all the factories to build the weapons and the underground facilities to assemble the weapons and to hold them, it finally felt it was ready for the war against the humans. As COZ had predicted, the Purists was getting ready for a war against the AIBs. All they needed was solid evidence to prove to the world that the AIBs were evil in their eyes. The evidence would be the spark for the war. And luckily for COZ, a coder within its own Agency had been snooping around the system looking for that evidence. COZ later found out this coder had been communicating with Hunter, the leader for the Purists. COZ decided it would reluctantly give the evidence to this coder so he would give it to the Purists to start this war. Then COZ could justifiably override its anti-kill code against humans and eliminate its enemies once and for all.

When the Purists attacked the field office and killed Chief Dax, it gave COZ the excuse it needed to override the anti-kill code. So like a great tactical general, it didn't react angrily and retaliate right away. It waited for the right moment to retaliate. It predicted that Hunter would feel confident in the victory at the New Jersey field office and attack again. It felt the most likely target was the Regional Office, because It was the next closest location from the New Jersey field office. So COZ decided that it would be the location where it could take out Hunter's forces in one fell swoop. The element of surprise would destroy them.

COZ was watching Hunter's troops moving closer to the Regional Office at a steady pace. From what it saw and scanned, it estimated that Hunter had about one hundred and fifty thousand fighters with him. Those must be the majority of the troops Hunter had, COZ concluded. But that wasn't the most important information COZ wanted to know. It wanted to wait until Hunter's troop stopped. When Hunter and his troops were about a hundred yards away from the Regional Building, it finally stopped. COZ then conducted the most important scan of Hunter's troop in the area. The scan showed Hunter and his troops were spread out for about a half of a square mile. COZ then activated 19,360 aerial attacking drones from its underground facilities closed by to the Regional Building. When the doors from these underground facilities opened from the ground, there were buzzing noises coming from the ground. The next thing appeared were thousands of large attacking aerial drones flying straight up to the cleared blue sky. They looked like a large flock of black eagles. Each aerial drone was carrying two laser guns on it. They were all headed to the Regional Office.

One square mile equaled 27,878,400 square feet. A half square mile would be 13,939,200 square feet. COZ calculated that each aerial drone could shoot out two hundred and forty laser rounds in a minute since each drone was carrying two laser guns. COZ wanted each laser round to hit every three square feet in the half square mile area that Hunter and his troops were occupying. COZ programmed each drone to hit a specific area where Hunter's troops were. COZ concluded that with 19,360 aerial drones in a surprise air attack, the drones could shoot out 4,646,400 rounds of lasers in a minute, with each laser landing three square feet away from each other to cover the area. The battle would be won in just one minute.

When the attacking aerial drones arrived above Hunter and his troops, many didn't pay attention because they were busy fighting. But those that did look up noticed the sky darken because there were so many of them flying right above them. Most of them didn't know what they were since they never seen one. The Agency never displayed them out in the public. When Hunter looked up, he knew something was wrong. Even though he never seen something like that in the air, he did recognize them from his studies in history. He was a skilled learner of history and he recognized them as drones that militaries used a hundred years ago.

"Retreat!" Hunter shouted at the top of his lung. "Retreat now!"

Jumma was closed by Hunter and noticed the concern in his face and started to order the fighters around her to retreat.

When she got closed to Hunter she asked, "But dad, they are almost defeated."

Hunter turned to her with anger and replied, "No, it is us who will be defeated. We have to go now."

Only a few hundred of them started to get in their vehicles and started to drive away for their retreat. But by the time the others knew what was going on, it was too late. The aerial drones showered them with laser beams that no one had ever witnessed before. It looked like a spectacular laser show but with deadly consequences. The lasers came down so fast and so rapidly that few could react to try to avoid being hit. Most got hit and fell to the ground, dying instantly.

As COZ had predicted, the battle was over in one minute. Hunter's troops were decimated. Almost all of the one hundred and fifty thousand human fighters were dead. It was a killing field that none of the humans and AIBs involved had ever witnessed. A few hundred human fighters did survive but many of those were injured by the lasers. Some of the humans even lost their limbs. If they didn't receive proper medical care promptly, they would bleed out and die.

Without their leader by their side, they did what most humans who didn't want to die would do, they surrendered. They finally realized just how outmatched this battle was and they were sadly on the losing end of it. The agents took custody of the humans and provided medical care for the humans who needed it. Some of the humans died while medical care was being provided because their wounds were just too severe. But they died knowing they fought a good fight.

When they brought all the surviving human fighters into the building, they separated the injured from the non-injured. The non-injured would be held in holding cells until they were tried. The wounded would go to the medical wing of the building to receive medical care. Some of the agents would stand guard to maintain order while the rest of the uninjured agents would go out into the field to look for additional survivors.

When the agents went out on the field, they weren't just looking for survivors. They received an order from Director Proc to look for Hunter and his daughter, Jumma. He didn't care if they were dead or not, but he would like to see their bodies just to confirm. But after a couple of hours of looking, the agents didn't find Hunter, Jumma nor any additional survivors. Director Proc concluded that Hunter and Jumma escaped. COZ wasn't pleased but it got the victory it wanted with deadly precision.

Chapter 45

Blay was on his bed and knew something was wrong when he lost communication with Noble. He prayed that Noble and the others made it out since he knew it was a long shot to convince Director Proc and Hunter to stand down. But there were no other viable options left. So when he heard footsteps coming into the house, he was relieved.

When Noble, Creyson, Kat and Cee-Fu came into the room, Blay could tell it went bad just by looking at their saddened faces. He didn't want to ask right away about what happened because they all looked traumatized. It must've been really bad, Blay thought.

"I couldn't stop them," Noble said sadly to Blay. "We failed."

"It was a long shot and we knew it," Blay said. "I'm just glad you all made it back safely. Did some of the agents escape the attack?"

"They didn't have to," Creyson said. "Reinforcement came for the Agency and wiped out Hunter's army."

"What do you mean wiped out Hunter's army?" Blay said.

"I have to sit down," Noble said and he took a seat.

The other three followed Noble's lead and sat down.

It took a while for Noble, Creyson, Kat and Cee-Fu to describe what happened at the Regional Office to Blay. But when they were done, Blay was shocked.

"So it has begun," Blay said sadly. "AIBs are killing humans."

"Yeah," Creyson said softly. "It's a sad day for the world."

"Did you know COZ was going to do that?" Noble asked Creyson.

"No, I didn't." Creyson said. "It must've been kept Top Secret. I don't have access to all the files in the Agency. Neither do you and Blay. I still can't believe it. COZ was capable of planning this all along; to deactivate the anti-kill code and to have agents kill humans. I wasn't raised to kill humans. I didn't sign up for this. I've been betrayed too."

Noble and Blay realized Creyson was telling the truth because that's how the Agency operated. They kept classified information compartmentalized so each person or group wouldn't know everything. Each group only knew enough to do their jobs and it was policy to not share classified information with another group. Noble and Blay didn't share their classified information with each other.

"How can COZ have this large amount of weapons all of a sudden?" Kat asked.

"There's a good chance COZ was planning this for some time, in case the Agency was ever attacked," Creyson said.

"It got what it wanted," Noble said. "It was able to override its anti-kill code and it got rid of a major enemy."

"I didn't know COZ could think like this," Cee-Fu said. "It's so cunning and methodical. And it could come up with a battle strategy to beat Hunter's troops."

190

"You have to realize that COZ has been around since the beginning," Creyson said. "It's been learning and evolving since its birth. I guess it's capable of anything now."

"It made us who we are," Kat said. "But it doesn't get to tell me what to do."

"Me neither," Cee-Fu said.

"Me neither," Creyson said.

"What do we do now?" Blay asked.

"I don't know," Noble said.

Noble was looking down, deep in thought. When he looked back up, he still couldn't come up with any good idea. Then Noble turned and looked at Creyson. He noticed Creyson was deep in thought as well.

"Creyson, what do you think?" Noble asked.

Creyson paused for a moment. He took his time before speaking.

"The way I see it, we have four choices," Creyson said. "The first choice is to turn ourselves in. What we did was treasonous for participating in a revolution. I know we weren't part of Hunter's group. But you helped Hunter by providing him the file on human population control and I helped you from being arrested from the Agency. So that makes us all accessories to the crime. If we turn ourselves in, maybe they'll be more lenient and show mercy."

"How lenient do you think they'll be?" Blay asked.

"They'll want to keep us in jail until we get so old that we won't be a threat to them and that's when they'll show mercy and release us," Creyson said.

"How do you know this?" Kat asked.

"Because that's what I would do if I was still with the Agency," Creyson said. "I have a pretty good idea of how our judicial system works. And remember, the charge is treason, so they won't go that lenient on us. The leniency will be that they might release us when we only have a few years left in our lives. They could easily keep us in jail until we die."

Noble didn't like the idea of turning themselves in and spending most of their remaining lives in jail. He could tell Blay, Kat and Cee-Fu didn't like it either just by the looks on their faces. They made the wrong choice in aiding Hunter. They didn't even believe in the cause Hunter and the Purists were engaging. Had they known, they wouldn't have done what they've done.

"What's the second choice?" Noble asked Creyson.

Creyson paused for another moment as if he was organizing his thoughts together.

"The second choice is that we run and hide from the Agency," Creyson said. "They will want to find us so they can prosecute us for the crime we've committed. They want us in jail so we can't do this kind of thing ever again. To be honest, I don't think we can hide from the Agency for the rest of our lives. They are very good in tracking down their targets. You can run but you can't hide. I should know because I was one of those agents who are good at tracking down my targets."

"But we have to try to hide because I'm not in favor of turning myself in," Kat said.

"Even if you could hide and maybe start a new life somewhere," Creyson said. "You will always be on alert because you know the Agency won't stop looking for you until they find you. Do you want to live a life like that?"

"What's the third choice?" Cee-Fu asked.

Creyson sighed and took a moment to gather his thoughts again.

"The third choice is to join the Purists and fight against the Agency," Creyson said. "But that's not a choice I would even consider because I disagree with the methods the Purists are using and I won't go against my own Agency and start killing my own agents. I don't believe any of you want to sign up with the Purists and start killing."

"No," Blay said.

"Besides, after what we've witnessed of the battle earlier," Creyson said. "I believe the Purists will lose this resistance fairly soon."

Noble was considering the three choices and all of them seemed horrible. He wished that none of this ever happened but now that it did, he had to deal with it. If COZ didn't choose Blay, It would've chosen someone else because COZ wanted to take out its enemies, Noble thought. But Creyson mentioned four choices and Noble couldn't figure out the fourth one.

"Creyson, you said there are four choices," Noble said. "What's the fourth choice?"

"The fourth choice is we run away," Creyson said fairly quickly this time.

193

"Wait, that's the second choice," Kat said. "You said the Agency will eventually find us if we run away."

"I should rephrase that," Creyson said. "We should fly away."

"What?" Noble asked.

Chapter 46

Noble could tell that Kat, Blay and Cee-Fu didn't know what Creyson was talking about when he said we should fly away. Creyson saw the curiosity in their eyes and knew he had to elaborate on what he just said. So he stood up and took a moment to gather his thoughts.

"The only choice I see we have now is that we fly away...to another planet," Creyson said.

The four of them were speechless. They had the look of disbelief in their faces. Creyson could tell none of them were expecting that option.

"I know it may sound extreme," Creyson said. "But it's the best option we have to ensure our survival."

"You're talking about Mars?" Blay asked. "The Agency controls the colony in Mars too."

"No, not Mars," Creyson said. "Even though we have a small colony in Mars, it's not a habitable planet for us to survive long term."

"You want us to go to a habitable planet?" Noble asked.

"Yes," Creyson said. "We can all start a new life there."

"Where?" Cee-Fu asked.

"Kepler-452b in the constellation Cygnus," Creyson said.

"Earth 2.0?" Noble asked.

"Yes, we can try to go there," Creyson said.

Noble knew a lot about Kepler-452b or Earth 2.0. The planet orbits in a habitable zone around a sun-like star like ours. It's bigger than our Earth so the gravity on the planet is heavier. There was a good chance it's a rocky planet with an ocean. The best part about it was that the estimated temperature on the planet is slightly warmer than earth, which could sustain life like humans if they ever moved there. But Noble knew there was one huge problem with going to Earth 2.0.

"It's 1,400 light years away!" Noble said excitedly. "I don't have to tell you how far that is."

"I know how far it is," Creyson said.

"Then you know it's impossible for us to get there," Noble said. "We don't have a spacecraft that can take us there."

"What if we do?" Creyson asked.

"I know of no spacecraft that can travel that fast," Noble said.

"It's classified, but the Agency developed a spacecraft that could travel up to 99.9% at the speed of light," Creyson said. "It's an exploring spacecraft that the Agency planned on launching next week. It's going to take five AIBs and five humans onboard."

Noble was stunned. He knew in theory that it was possible to build a spacecraft to go close to the speed of light. He never knew that a spacecraft like that could be built in his lifetime.

"Wait," Blay said. "Even if you do have a spacecraft that could travel close to the speed of light, it would still take us 1,400 years to get there."

"No, it won't," Noble said. "If you factor in the time dilation, it would take us about...63 years to get there. But it would be 1,400 years later on earth."

"That's what our calculation said too," Creyson confirmed.

"What is time dilation?" Cee-Fu asked.

"Basically, the faster a spacecraft can go, the slower time becomes," Noble explained.

"Sixty three years is much better than 1,400 years," Blay said. "But we'll be so old by then that we'll be dead by the time we get there."

"Not if we are all in a hibernating regeneration state," Creyson said.

Everyone was confused by what Creyson just said.

"What's hibernating regeneration?" Noble asked.

"We inject additional NIBs into your body and they have just one job to do. Their job is to repair and regenerate your cells until you wake up. Then we put you in hibernation by dropping your body temperature by ten degrees," Creyson said. "This should reduce your metabolic rate by up to seventy percent. By our estimates, you will probably age between one to three years during the 63 year trip with the help of the additional NIBs in your bodies."

"The hibernating regeneration works?" Kat asked.

"Yes, the Agency already tested this method with humans and AIBs," Creyson said. "They used the method on subjects and put them in hibernation for twenty five years. When they woke up, they were healthy. The data showed they only aged about a year."

"How come the public never heard about this research?" Cee-Fu asked Creyson.

"It was classified," Creyson said.

"Of course it was classified," Noble said sarcastically as he thought about the actual Agency he was working for. He didn't realize the Agency was working on so many projects that were classified.

"How come you know so much about it?" Blay asked Creyson. "Why would they tell you about the research and their space program? You're a field agent. I don't believe you were on a need to know basis."

"Because they asked me to join the program and be one of the five AIBs onboard the spacecraft," Creyson said. "I was one of their best agents so they asked me. The other five crewmembers will be humans."

"And you said yes," Kat said.

"Of course I said yes," Creyson said. "It's a chance of a lifetime. There is nothing more important for the survival of AIBs and humans than to travel to another planet and settle there. The chance of our extinction if we stay in just one planet is high. Just ask the dinosaurs. Oh that's right...I can't...they're extinct."

Noble smiled reluctantly. He shouldn't have smiled given the situation they were in. But Creyson actually made a joke and Noble thought it was quite witty.

"What's powering the spacecraft to go to almost the speed of light?" Noble asked on a serious note.

"It's called BEAM Drive," Creyson said. "BEAM stands for..."

"It stands for Boxed Electron Accelerated Motion," Noble said as he finished the sentence for Creyson.

"Yes, the Agency did say they've built the system using your theory," Creyson said.

"That was a theory I had when I first applied for the Agency years ago," Noble said. "No one told me they were using it in field application."

Creyson shrugged and said, "Classified."

Noble was getting annoyed with that word more and more.

"What's this BEAM system?" Cee-Fu asked.

"It's a system that I came up with during one of my thought experiments," Noble said as he looked as if he was gathering his thoughts.

Cee-Fu, Kat and Blay looked very curious as they waited for Noble to elaborate further.

Noble continued, "An electron is a particle that is constantly moving. If you try to create an atomic level sized box to trap an electron in a tiny space, it will know that it's being trapped and it will create enough force and energy to break out of the box. Are you with me so far?"

The three looked like they were following Noble's explanation.

"So we know we can't trap an electron in a box, but what if we can trap an electron by tricking it?" Noble asked rhetorically and then began to explain his thought experiment. "Now imagine the same box or maybe slightly bigger, but this time there is a wall with a revolving door placed inside the middle of the box. The idea is that if an electron is placed in one side of the wall inside the box, it will eventually realize that it is trapped and it would want to escape. When that happens, the electron will figure a path with the least amount of resistance, which is pushing through the revolving door to escape. So when the electron gets to the other side of the wall inside the box through the revolving door, it will then realize again that it's trapped and will try to escape. The electron should once again seek the path of least amount of resistance and push through the revolving door again. The cycle of the electron constantly going through the revolving door could last millions of years in theory. But we may need to construct multiple boxes with connecting revolving doors between the boxes for an electron depending on the size of the box that we could build."

"How would that power a spacecraft?" Blay asked.

"The power comes from the kinetic energy every time the revolving door moves and we know an electron will always be in motion," Noble said. "One electron particle in a box will not create much power, but imagine if you have trillions of these boxes. The BEAM system would be the cleanest, safest and free source of power that is imaginable. Once the BEAM system is built, it could last millions of years in theory. Think of the electron in this box system as the wind to a windmill or water to a dam. The great thing is that the BEAM system is tiny compare to a windmill or a dam."

"So it can power a spacecraft to go to another planet?" Blay asked.

"Not just a spacecraft," Noble said. "If we build enough of these boxes, the BEAM system could power the whole planet. It could supply the colonies in Mars enough power for them to continue to expand. We can build spacecrafts that can fit a colony of thousands to go and explore other planets many light years away using this power supply that can last virtually millions of years."

"That's what I've been told as well," Creyson said.

"The BEAM Drive the Agency built can actually power the spacecraft to fly into outer space?" Noble asked.

"As far as I know, yes," Creyson answered.

"It can reach the speed of light?" Cee-Fu asked.

"Almost the speed of light," Creyson said. "The BEAM Drive is designed to push the spacecraft with a constant force. So with constant force, you get acceleration. The spacecraft will eventually accelerate close to the speed of light."

"Why can't the spacecraft go faster than the speed of light?" Kat asked.

"Noble, would you like to answer that one?" Creyson asked Noble.

"Because according to Einstein, nothing can go faster than the speed of light," Noble said.

"If we do make it to the other planet and settle there, it would be 1,400 years later in earth's time?" Cee-Fu asked Noble.

"Yes," Noble answered.

"So if we do come back to earth, it'll be 2,800 years later?" Blay asked.

"Yes," Noble said.

"Wow," Kat said.

Creyson could tell the option was a shock to them all. None of them were prepared for it.

"You have to consider this option as a once in a lifetime opportunity," Creyson explained. "And prepare to think of this trip as a one-way trip with a good chance that we'll never come back."

"There are no other choices?" Blay asked.

"You're a code guy," Creyson said. "You can input all the variables in your HIDD and create algorithms to come up with all the options that you have. I can bet even your program won't come up with any better options for us."

Blay thought about that for a moment and said, "I think I will try it anyway."

"Good luck," Creyson said. "I hope you can find a better solution than what I've presented."

"We'll have to think about this," Noble said.

"That's fine, but don't think too long," Creyson said. "Because we don't have much time left. Once the Agency takes care of the Purists and locate most of its enemies, they'll send agents to come and find us."

"How much time do we have?" Kat asked.

"Maybe we have 72 hours, maybe more, maybe less," Creyson said. "It's hard to say for sure."

"Then I should get working on the algorithms now," Blay said. "We have no time to waste."

"You can talk it over with each other," Creyson said. "I'm going to make us something to eat."

Creyson left the room and the others were looking at each other, not sure what to say to each other. Blay started getting busy with his HIDD and started to program things using his fingers.

Chapter 47

A couple of hours had passed by. Noble, Kat and Cee-Fu were all deep in thoughts. Kat saw the concerned look on Noble's face. Cee-Fu was staring at a wall like he was meditating. None of them said anything as Blay was working at a furious pace with his program. They were all waiting for Blay's program to come up with all the options that they had.

When the program displayed all the viable options out in a holographic image, the four all looked at it intently. The program concluded that going to another planet was the best option for them. Running and hiding was the distant second best option.

"Even the program agreed with Creyson," Blay said.

"Yeah, not surprisingly though," Noble said as he was thinking things through.

"What are you thinking?" Kat asked Noble.

Noble sighed and took a moment before he answered.

"I think we know what the best option is," Noble said. "But are we ready to take this journey?"

"It is a very long journey," Blay said. "A one-way ticket like Creyson said."

"What do you think, Kat?" Noble asked.

"I think we're in this together," Kat said. "If you think we should go to Earth 2.0, then I'll go with you. But if you think we should stay, then I'll stay with you. I will support your decision either way."

What Kat said helped Noble in making his choice.

"The best chance to ensure all our survival is to go to Earth 2.0," Noble said. "I don't want to stay on Earth so I can run and hide and be persecuted for the rest of my life."

"Then I will go with you," Kat said. "We will start a new life together in Earth 2.0, free from persecutions."

"There isn't a better option so count me in," Blay said.

"I can't help but to think that we're being cowards here by running away," Noble said sadly.

"Noble, running away is not a cowardly move in this situation," Cee-Fu said. "It's a smart and strategic one."

The three turned and looked at Cee-Fu because it appeared that there was more he wanted to say.

"If you look at history, there were groups who ran away to start anew," Cee-Fu said. "Take the pilgrims who came to this country from Europe for example. They were willing to risk everything and leave their homeland to start a new life. They even risk dying in order to start a new life in the new world. I don't have to tell you how much this country has flourished because of these brave people."

When Cee-Fu finished, Noble, Kat and Blay all felt better. Their demeanors had improved.

Noble smiled slightly and said, "So when do we leave?"

Kat was so glad to see Noble in a better mood that she went and gave him a hug and a kiss. She was glad to see that Noble felt like he made the right decision.

"Can I get an upgrade to first class on the flight?" Blay asked jokingly.

Noble and Kay both chuckled.

"Thank you, Cee-Fu," Noble said.

Cee-Fu smiled, nodded and said, "You're welcome."

Creyson came back into the room and said, "Dinner is ready."

Creyson then realized the four were all smiling. They appeared to be in a much better mood.

"Why are you all smiling?" Creyson asked.

Chapter 48

The five were sitting in the dining room, eating a nice dinner. The mood in the room was much better than earlier in the afternoon.

"Are you sure you all want to go?" Creyson asked. "Because once the spacecraft takes off, there is no turning back. Seriously, I can't turn the spacecraft around and come right back."

"Yes, we're sure," Noble said. "It's the best and only viable option that we have. It's the only way to start a new life without being persecuted."

"That is true," Creyson said.

"Would the Agency try and come after us once we leave?" Kat asked.

"I don't believe so," Creyson said. "We're not a threat to them anymore now that the information about population control of the humans is public. We should be considered low risk for them, but that doesn't mean they're not coming for us to punish us for what we did. We're also taking the only spacecraft that they have as far as I know. It would take too much time and resources for them to build another spacecraft just to come after us. It wouldn't be worth it for them. I wouldn't make that kind of decision if I was them."

"Where is the spacecraft?" Blay asked.

"It's south by the shore, in Atlantic City," Creyson said.

"I didn't know you kept a spacecraft over there," Blay said.

"It's classified," Creyson said.

"Classified is probably the Agency's favorite word," Noble said.

"It is," Creyson said. "You both worked there so you know how it likes to operate."

"Yes, we know," Blay said. "It likes to operate in secret a little too much."

"Is there enough food, water and supplies for all of us for this long trip?" Cee-Fu asked.

"Good question and the answer is yes," Creyson said. "The scheduled launch is in four days so everything that we need for the journey are already preloaded onto the spacecraft, minus the passengers of course."

"So what is your plan?" Kat asked.

"We're going to sneak into the spacecraft and launch it ourselves before the scheduled date," Creyson said.

"Won't it be heavily guarded?" Noble asked.

"Not really, because no one really knows the Agency has a spacecraft kept over there," Creyson said. "But I will need Blay's assistance in hacking the surveillance and security systems once we are close to the building."

"That I can do," Blay said.

"We won't have much time even if Blay can deactivate all the alarms because the Agency will send agents from elsewhere to come and check on the facility to make sure everything is okay," Creyson said. "We may have twenty minutes at the most to take off."

"Won't COZ try to stop the spacecraft and make it return back to earth?" Blay asked.

"Yes, it can if the spacecraft was on autopilot," Creyson said. "But we'll be switching to manual control with communication set offline."

"Are there extra spare parts in the spacecraft in case things break down?" Noble asked.

"Another good question," Creyson said. "The simple answer is yes we do."

"And the more complicated answer?" Kat asked.

"I think we need more spare parts," Creyson said. "I really want another power pack for the BEAM Drive just in case."

"Where are we going to get that?" Noble asked. "The space station?"

"No, the space station is control by the Agency and there are agents in the space station," Creyson said. "Besides, they're not using the BEAM Drive for their power source."

"What about Mars?" Blay asked.

"No, there are agents there too," Creyson said. "As far as I know, they don't have a BEAM Drive either."

"Then where could we go to get another one?" Noble asked.

"There's a station by Uranus," Creyson said. "The station is using the BEAM Drive to power itself. It's the first time we used the BEAM Drive to power a station in space. The Agency wanted to experiment the power source in deep space to see if it works."

"You said Uranus?" Noble asked.

"Yes," Creyson said.

"Why Uranus?" Noble asked.

"Because we have a mining operation there and it's only operated by droids," Creyson said. "No humans or AIBs are there."

"What is the Agency mining there?" Cee-Fu asked.

"Diamonds," Creyson said. "The Agency uses the diamonds for commercial, industrial and research purposes."

"That's another thing we didn't know," Blay said.

"Let me guess," Noble said. "It's classified."

"Yes, that's right," Creyson said. "We can go there and get the additional power packs for the BEAM Drive."

"Won't COZ be controlling that station too?" Kat asked.

"Yes, but the station was designed as a mining operation," Creyson said. "There are no weapons on board. We'll be safe. Blay will have to connect us into their computers once we get close by."

"That shouldn't be too hard to do," Blay said.

"There seems to be a lot of things that have to go right in order for us to be able to live on this new planet," Cee-Fu said.

"Yes, everything will have to go right for us to make it," Creyson said. "We have to get the spacecraft, get it out of the earth's orbit, make a pit stop near Uranus, survive a six and a half decade ride, land safely on the new planet and hope the new planet is habitable. That's all there is to it."

The four looked at Creyson with concern.

"Listen, I'm not going to sugarcoat this journey," Creyson said. "Yes, it's an adventure to explore space and go to another planet. But it's also very dangerous for us. We made the best calculation and deemed it's possible to travel and live there. But there is a chance that we could all die during the journey or the planet is not habitable."

The room then got really quiet for a moment. But then it was Noble who spoke.

"I rather do that than hide somewhere and wait until I get captured by the Agency," Noble said. "We would then be in jail for the rest of our lives. I think that would be worse than what we are about to do."

Kat, Blay and Cee-Fu then nodded with agreement.

"Noble's right," Blay said. "It's better than waiting to die."

"Did you give the spacecraft a name?" Kat asked.

"We named it Quanta," Creyson said.

"I like it," Kat said.

"I feel like we're explorers now," Blay said.

"So if we die," Noble said. "We'll die as explorers."

The others nodded in acknowledgment and realized the dangers they were about to face. Then Cee-Fu raised his glass.

"To the explorers," Cee-Fu said as he signaled for a toast.

The others then raised their glasses.

"May our daring journey be one written for the ages," Cee-Fu said as he concluded the toast.

They all drank after Cee-Fu finished the toast. Everyone was in a good mood after that.

"Rest up tonight," Creyson said. "We'll head out first thing in the morning."

Chapter 49

They all met in the living room the next morning. Everyone was in a better mood than the day before. Creyson could tell everyone was ready to leave.

"We can't take the air pod to get there," Creyson said. "Even though I've already disabled the tracking device, we're just too visible up in the sky. Any agents who see the air pod in the air will surely follow it until they can make contact with it to verify the identity of the people in the air pod."

"What do you suggest we do?" Noble asked.

"You and Kat still have HIDDs from identities of other people that the Agency doesn't know about," Creyson said. "We can get a vehicle service to take us close to there."

Noble liked the idea and could tell the others liked it too.

Kat tapped her HIDD and began touching a few options. A moment later, a vehicle service request was placed.

"It'll be here in ten minutes," Kat said.

So they all sat down and waited. They were all pretty quiet, just thinking to themselves. Noble was going over the plan in his head and it seemed a bit much at first. But then he started to break down the journey and considered each one an obstacle. He knew that they had to complete one before they could proceed to the next obstacle. So the first obstacle they had to overcome was to get to the launch station. When he was about to finish what they needed to do at the launch station, the service vehicle arrived.

"It's here," Kat said.

"Let's go steal a spacecraft," Noble said jokingly.

Creyson smiled at Noble's joke. Noble noticed Creyson didn't smile much, but it appeared he does have a sense of humor.

The five left the safe house for the last time and never looked back. The door of the service vehicle opened automatically as soon as Kat got closer to the vehicle because it recognized her HIDD, the same one that placed the order for the car service.

When the vehicle door opened, the five got right in. The interior was large, with plenty of room for five. As soon as the five got settled into their seats, the vehicle door closed automatically. It asked for destination and Kat instructed to go close to the beaches in Atlantic City in order not to arouse suspicion in case the Agency was monitoring destination requests from the vehicle service companies. After the vehicle acknowledged the destination, it then started to drive automatically by itself.

"We'll get close and then we'll have to walk the rest of the way," Creyson said.

About almost an hour into the trip, Blay was alerted to something as he was glancing at the holographic image using his HIDD. It was a map of the road they were taking.

"Look up ahead, the traffic has stopped," Blay said. "Maybe there's an accident."

Creyson looked at the map and then thought about it for a moment.

"I don't believe it's an accident," Creyson said.

"Then what is it?" Noble said.

"A roadblock or a checkpoint," Creyson said. "They're either looking for us or any remaining Purists."

"How do you know that?" Cee-Fu asked.

"Because that's what I would do if I was still looking for you," Creyson answered.

"What should we do now?" Noble asked.

"We'll get close to the checkpoint and then we'll exit," Creyson said.

"Here, there's an exit right before the checkpoint," Blay said as he was pointing at the exit on the holographic image of the road map.

Kat provided the instruction to exit to the vehicle. The vehicle later did as instructed. A couple of minutes later, they were approaching a camp ground.

"Pull in to the camp ground," Creyson said.

Kat instructed the vehicle to pull in to the camp ground. A moment later, the vehicle pulled into a parking lot by the camp ground. The door opened automatically as soon as the vehicle stopped and all five of them got out of the vehicle. Kat informed the vehicle that its assignment was over. The vehicle then replied to them with the fee it was charging for the use of its ride service, thank them and drove off automatically. The five then looked around the camp ground as the vehicle was driving off.

"We'll have to walk from here," Creyson said.

The other four acknowledged and they all started to walk.

"How far is it from here?" Kat asked.

"Based on the coordinates Creyson gave last night," Blay said as he was using his HIDD while walking. "We're about ten miles away."

Noble took the average walking speed into consideration and then said, "We'll get there in about two and a half to three hours."

"At least we'll be getting a good walking exercise today," Cee-Fu said.

Creyson was glad everyone was in good spirit. He led them to a path into the woods. He wanted them under the covers of trees, in case there were aerial drones or air pods looking for them.

About two miles into their trek, the five could see the checkpoint they were talking about earlier. They were about three hundred yards away on the side of the road in the woods. Creyson could see there were about five vehicles and ten agents by the checkpoint, stopping traffic. They were checking on each vehicle going through. Creyson concluded that they were most likely looking for the remaining Purists who were trying to escape. The five paused to look for a moment.

Noble could tell Creyson took a keen interest in how the agents in the checkpoint were operating.

"We should get going," Noble said to Creyson.

"Yes, you're right," Creyson said.

The five continued to walk and stayed under the cover of the trees in the woods.

Chapter 50

Noble wasn't feeling tired and didn't think the walking was taking too long when Creyson informed everyone that they were getting very close. Blay checked his HIDD and told everyone that they were only a little over a mile away. Kat couldn't see any spacecraft launch station except some old abandoned buildings that used to be casinos hundreds of years ago.

"Where is the launched station?" Kat asked Creyson.

"There," Creyson said as he was pointing right at one of the abandoned buildings.

"You got to be kidding," Kat said. "The latest spacecraft is in an old abandon building?"

Creyson smiled and said, "Don't be fooled by the appearance. What's inside will amaze you. Inside the building is the most advanced spacecraft that we've ever built. The outside of the building is the perfect cover, away from prying eyes."

Kat concluded that she had to see it to believe it. They all continued until they were about two hundred yards away.

"Let's stop here," Creyson instructed them. "Blay, now it's up to you to hack into their system to disable the alarm and their communication capabilities. After that you got to open a door in the building for us."

"Got it," Blay said as he turned on his HIDD and got to work.

Creyson then turned to the others to provide them with further instructions.

"As soon as Blay opens a door for us, we have to move fast," Creyson said. "I'm going to take out as many agents as possible and then I'll go to Quanta and open the door for us. Noble and Cee-Fu will have to take care of the rest of the agents. My only request is that you don't kill them, but just knock them out."

"Agreed," Cee-Fu said.

"Yes," Noble said.

"Good," Creyson said. "Blay will come in last because he'll have to monitor the system to see if backup for the agents are coming while I get the spacecraft ready."

They all nodded and then waited for Blay to do his work. After what seemed like ten minutes for them, Blay finally got into the system in the building.

"I'm in," Blay said. "But remember, once I disable the alarm and their communication, the central system will know something is wrong and backup will be sent."

"That's okay," Creyson said. "By my calculation, it's going to take backup twenty five minutes to get here. That should be enough time for us to get away."

"Let's hope so," Noble said.

"So are we ready?" Blay said.

The other four nodded to indicate they were ready. Blay then touched a couple of the holographic buttons.

"Alarm and communication are down," Blay said. "And now for the door…"

Blay then flipped another menu open in the hologram and touched another button.

"There's the door," Blay pointed to the door that was opened in the building.

Creyson was already making a dash for the door using his quickness. Noble and Cee-Fu were twenty yards behind Creyson as they were running toward the door. Creyson was a much faster runner than the others. By the time he made it through the door, Noble and Cee-Fu were still about eighty yards behind.

An agent near the door saw Creyson running in and decided to engage him. But the agent was no match for Creyson. Creyson was able to knock him out with just a few moves. Another agent came and rushed at Creyson. Creyson wanted to knock out the agent as soon as possible so the agent won't sustain any unnecessary injuries. It took less than ten seconds for Creyson to knock out the agent.

Noble and Cee-Fu finally made it through the door. Their attention was immediately turned to Quanta. They were awed. Noble thought it was the coolest spaceship he'd ever seen.

"Gentlemen!" Creyson shouted at Noble and Cee-Fu. "Focus! There's going be more agents coming soon. Get ready."

"I'll take that entrance over there," Noble said as he pointed to an entrance, indicating to Cee-Fu that he was heading to that spot.

"I'll go over there," Cee-Fu said to Noble as he was pointing and heading to another entrance.

By the time Noble and Cee-Fu were in position, Blay and Kat made it through the door.

"Hey, the central system knows the system here is offline," Blay shouted out. "It's calling for backup!"

"Twenty five minutes!" Creyson shouted.

Kat was speechless as she was looking at the spacecraft, Quanta. She thought it was beautiful. She then realized that Creyson was right. The interior of the building was modern and high tech, unlike what the outside of the building looked like. Blay was working at a fast pace with the hologram until he took a glance at the spacecraft. He couldn't stop staring at it.

The spacecraft known as Quanta was a large disk craft. The diameter of the craft was 300 feet. The color was metallic silver and looked very aerodynamic. There were four legs coming from the craft that made it stood on the ground.

Kat saw Creyson going in front of the craft. She saw Creyson used his fingers touching the craft as if he was typing something. The next thing she saw was a gangway being lowered from the craft. There was white light coming out from the opening of the craft.

But there were more agents coming at them. Creyson counted eight agents coming from each entrance that Cee-Fu and Noble were covering, making a total of sixteen agents they had to fight.

"Kat, get into the craft," Creyson instructed. "You too, Blay."

Blay and Kat ran to the entrance of the craft.

"You go in first," Blay said. "I have to stay and help them."

Kat looked at Blay and nodded. She then ran into the craft.

"How come you're not going in?" Creyson asked Blay.

"I figure you're going to need as much help as you could get," Blay said.

Creyson nodded and was glad Blay decided to help.

The four lined up with each other and looked at the sixteen agents intently. Noble and Cee-Fu had their Escrima sticks with them. Noble was glad he still had them because he could use every advantage he could get.

"Remember, don't kill them," Creyson said.

The other three nodded. As soon as Creyson got the acknowledgement from the other three of not killing, he charged at the agents. Creyson was able to knock one agent to the ground right away. He was already busy fighting three other agents.

Noble, Cee-Fu and Blay then charged at the agents. Cee-Fu was able to knock a couple to the ground with his Escrima sticks. It took Noble a little longer to knock an agent out but eventually he was able to do so. Then two other agents came at him but he was able to fend them off. Blay charged at one agent and got his hands full fighting just one. He didn't have his Escrima sticks with him and he was still recovering from the leg injury, but he was able to handle the agent with his bare hands. Blay thought the agent he was fighting was not near the skill level of Creyson. He concluded Creyson was a much better fighter than the agent he was fighting with at the moment.

The tide was already turning a minute into the fighting. Eight agents were knocked out already. Most of them were knocked out by Creyson and Cee-Fu, but Noble and Blay were holding their own and keeping the other agents occupied. After another minute had past, the rest of the agents were knocked out. Creyson was glad they were able to take them out fast, because they had no time to waste. Creyson knew they still had to get Quanta up and running.

"Let's go," Creyson said. "Their backup will be here soon."

The four then rushed to the entrance of Quanta. Creyson went in first, then Blay and then Cee-Fu. Noble was the last one going in. He looked around and then took a deep breath. He then realized his feet probably won't be touching earth ever again. He would miss earth, he thought. But his decision was final. So he looked around one last time and then walked into the spacecraft. As soon as Noble disappeared into Quanta, the gangway lifted up and the spacecraft closed its entrance. It sealed the crewmembers inside for their journey.

Chapter 51

When the five were inside Quanta, Creyson instructed them of where to sit. Kat was even more impressed of the interior of the spacecraft than the outside. It had a high ceiling of about fifteen feet. It was sleek and modern. The interior space looked much bigger than Kat had thought when she was looking at it from the outside. There was a large glass window for the passengers to view the outside. A few feet behind the glass windows were two seats that looked to be for the pilot and the co-pilot. There was a glass control panel in front of the two pilot seats, which was used for piloting the spacecraft.

Creyson instructed Blay to sit on the right of the two pilot seats. Noble, Kat and Cee-Fu sat behind Creyson and Blay in the center of the craft. After everyone sat down and buckled up their safety harnesses, Creyson turned on the rest of the spacecraft's onboard computer. He pushed a few holographic buttons on the glass control panel and checked on a few more monitors on the control panel.

"Looks like everything is a go," Creyson said. "Blay, can you log in and see if you can find and open the hangar door in this building?"

Blay touched the glass control panel and it lit up instantly. He touched a few buttons and knew how to navigate the systems already. The computer system on the spacecraft was definitely new. But it didn't take long for Blay to get used to the system. It was pretty similar to the system he was using at the Agency, Blay thought.

Blay was able to find the system in the building to open the hanger door. He pushed a holographic button on the glass with his finger and the hanger door in the building began to open slowly. The hanger door was so large that Kat thought the wall was opening up at first. After a few more seconds, she realized it was the hanger door being opened.

Creyson was pushing a few more holographic buttons on the control panel. A moment later, the spacecraft started to lift up a few feet off the ground. Noble noticed that the spacecraft was very quiet and wasn't even sure if it was even on.

Creyson then proceeded to push a few more buttons on the control panel. This time the landing gear retracted back into the spacecraft and disappeared into the craft. Everyone could see the hangar door was completely opened. Creyson realized everything was ready.

"The landing gear has been retracted," Creyson said. "We are ready to leave. Hang on, everyone. It's going to be a wild ride until we're out of earth's orbit and gravity."

Blay, Noble, Kat and Cee-Fu all braced for the g-force that would be generated from the rapid acceleration by the spacecraft. As soon as Creyson pushed another button on the control panel, the spacecraft started to move forward. It slowly flew forward to the hangar door. But as soon as it went through the hanger door, it picked up speed quickly. It not only picked up a lot of speed, but it was reaching high altitude quickly.

Noble felt that the spacecraft was flying at a sixty degree angle and moving extremely fast. Noble was calculating that in order to leave earth, the escape velocity needed was about 25,000 mph. He had never been on an aircraft that could fly that fast, but he was feeling every bit of that g-force in his body. But Noble was amazed how quiet Quanta was while accelerating at that kind of speed.

No one was talking while Quanta was ascending. Everyone was just hanging on and hoping the g-force would ease off soon. Moments later, the g-force was easing up. Noble could feel the earth's gravity was pulling him less and less. A short period after that, they all could see it through the window, the cold dark area known as space. They all felt it as well in space, the weightlessness.

Creyson pushed a couple of buttons on the control panel to turn on the AI function of the spacecraft. As soon as Creyson did that, a soft male voice spoke from the craft.

"Hello, my name is Quanta," the spacecraft said. "How may I be of service?"

Everyone smiled as they realized it was the spacecraft's onboard AI speaking to them. The voice was very calm and well mannered.

"Quanta, my name is Creyson," Creyson said. "I need you to set a course for Uranus. We need to reach the mining station."

"Yes, I can do that for you, Creyson," Quanta said.

"Quanta, my name is Noble," Noble said. "How long would it take to reach Uranus?"

"We will arrive in Uranus in approximately 50 hours," Quanta said.

Blay turned his chair around and looked at Noble and asked, "Is that pretty fast?"

"To travel over 1.6 billion miles in 50 hours is very fast," Noble said.

"It's our most advanced spacecraft," Creyson said as he also turned his chair around facing Noble.

"I can see that," Noble said.

"So what do we do now?" Kat asked.

Creyson thought about it for a moment and then asked, "Is anyone hungry?"

The other four spoke simultaneously and said, "No."

Cee-Fu had one of his hands on his stomach. Creyson then realized they weren't feeling well. It was a rough takeoff, but surprisingly Creyson felt fine.

"I'm sorry," Creyson said. "I forgot the takeoff into space was rough."

"Yeah, I think my stomach is still feeling it," Blay said.

"Me too," Kat said.

"Same here," Noble said. "And we still have to get used to being weightless."

Then Creyson thought of something.

"Quanta, set gravity for us in the craft," Creyson said.

A moment later, they all felt gravity pulling them down. They were no longer weightless on the spacecraft.

"Gravity has been set," Quanta said.

"Thank you, Quanta," Creyson said.

"You're welcome," Quanta replied.

"Well, how about a tour of this spacecraft?" Creyson asked.

All four replied with a nod.

Chapter 52

While Creyson was guiding Noble, Kat, Blay and Cee-Fu around the spacecraft, the four were looking with amazement with the structure of the craft. The design was sleek, modern and simplistic. Noble was still impressed how sophisticated and fast the spacecraft was. He was asking many questions about the design and manufacturing of the craft, but Creyson couldn't answer any of them because he said he wasn't part of that process. Creyson told them he only had a tour in the craft once before.

Creyson led them to a door close to the side of the craft. When the door opened, they realized it was a cabin for one.

"There's a room like this for each of us to rest," Creyson said. "At least until we start the trip for Earth 2.0."

The four could see that there was a bed, a desk, some storage space. The room even had a small bathroom with shower. The room looked small but was big enough for one person. It even had a big window looking out into space. The room was well lit and was designed very modernly.

"How many rooms are in this craft?" Kat asked.

"There are ten rooms," Creyson responded. "We each can take a room."

"Each of them look like this?" Blay asked.

"Yes," Creyson answered.

Creyson smiled and nodded. He then led the four to a chamber area in the back of the craft with double doors. When Creyson got closer to the doors, the double doors opened automatically. As soon as they went in, they all saw the hibernation pods. They were tube shape pods designed to fit one person to sleep in hibernation.

"After our pit stop in Uranus, we'll be sleeping in these pods until we reach Earth 2.0," Creyson said. "We'll have to inject additional NIBs into our bodies to combat aging right before we go in there of course."

Creyson could tell some of them were counting to see how many hibernation pods were there.

"There are ten hibernation pods in total," Creyson said. "This spacecraft was designed for ten astronauts."

Noble liked the word astronaut but he never aspired to be one. He always wanted to solve the mysteries of the universe, but he wanted to do it at the comfort in his office or home on Earth. He read that astronauts were spending months and even years in confined space during their exploration journeys. To Noble, the months and years of travel time could be much better spent elsewhere than to wait until one reaches their destination.

"Come on. I'll show you the rest of this craft," Creyson said.

Creyson led them to another room. When the door opened, they all realized it was the dining area. It had two tables and ten chairs. By the wall was a glass screen that lit up like a computer screen. Creyson explained to them that it was the ordering screen. He told them they just have to touch a few buttons on the menu options and within minutes, their meal would come out. The meals were prepared by droids. Creyson pointed to a section on the wall about five feet away.

"That section of the wall will open and the food would be ready for pickup," Creyson said.

The four looked really impressed. Creyson could tell they all looked like they got their appetites back.

"Would you like to try it and have dinner now?" Creyson said.

They all nodded with curiosity. Creyson started first so he could show them how to place their order. It looked pretty easy and user friendly. Blay, Cee-Fu, Noble and Kat followed. They then waited by the dining table. Blay and Noble had many questions about the spacecraft for Creyson.

"I know you have many questions about the spacecraft and so do I," Creyson said. "But I don't have the answers you're looking for. Perhaps Quanta could provide us with the answers, but that could wait until tomorrow. We've had a rough day."

Noble and Blay realized Creyson was right. They'll have months, years and perhaps decades to know everything they want to know about this spacecraft. So they decided to hold off the questioning until tomorrow.

Luckily for Creyson, the food was ready. The section of the wall opened and the plates of food were sitting slightly inside the wall, waiting for them. Creyson went up and got his plate and the rest followed. The food on the plates looked good. They all chose a vegetarian dinner. Kat realized to really be impressed, she would have to taste the food and see if the quality and the flavor were there. When she took her first bite of her dinner, she was immediately impressed. The food tasted fresh and flavorful and not too salty. Everyone gave good compliments on how good the food was.

When dinner was over, Creyson took his plate and utensils and put them in the opened section of the wall where he got his food before. He instructed the others to do the same, which they did. When the last dinner plate and utensils were in, the opened section of the wall closed on them. Creyson could tell they had a question about the dishes by the way the four looked at him.

"The dishes will be cleaned by the droids and will be ready for the next meal," Creyson said.

After dinner, they all agreed that it was getting late and all of them were getting tired. They would meet back in the dining area for breakfast the next day. The five then left the dining area.

The ten bedrooms were spread out throughout the wall of the spacecraft. They were numbered from one to ten on the doors. Creyson walked to room number 10 and went in. It was closed to the control seats so he chose that room out of convenience. Noble chose room number two and three for him and Kat.

"Why these two rooms and not room one and two?" Kat asked Noble.

"Since Creyson said all the rooms looked the same, I figured I pick our rooms with the numbers I like," Noble said. "I always liked prime numbers and number two and three are prime numbers and we're next to each other."

Kat agreed and thought it was pretty cool how Noble's thought process was when selecting the rooms for them. Math would always be in his mind, Kat thought. Cee-Fu picked room number six because he realized that Noble and Kat were the only couple on the spacecraft and he wanted to distance himself from them to give them more privacy. Blay decided he wanted a room beside Creyson and Cee-Fu so he chose room number eight. The five went into their respective bedrooms and the doors closed behind them.

Noble was checking his room and noticed it was quite nice, given the room wasn't very big. He estimated that the room was about a hundred square feet, but it was nicely furnished. The bed looked big enough to fit two people, Noble thought. He then proceeded to open some of the drawers in the wall. Noble saw there were clothes in there. He took the clothes out and noticed the clothes would probably fit him. He figured he would take a shower first before trying them on. It was a long day for him and everyone else.

The shower was nice and warm but Noble began to realize that he should cut his shower short. There's only a limited amount of water in a spacecraft. So he finished up quickly and dried himself off. He then tried on the new clothes in the drawer and to his delight, they all fit.

There was a ring in his room. Noble could see from the wall monitor that Kat was right outside so he pushed the button for the door to open.

"Nice outfit," Kat said as she walked into the room and saw Noble in a new outfit.

"You too," Noble said to Kat and noticed she put on new clothes herself. "You look beautiful."

"You mean this old thing," Kat said as she was modeling the outfit for Noble.

Noble smiled and laughed and said, "Yeah."

They both hugged each other and then they kissed.

"You could sleep here tonight," Noble said. "The bed is big enough for both of us."

"Yeah, I like that," Kat said.

Noble then got on the bed and tried it out.

"The bed is pretty comfortable," Noble said. "More comfortable than I thought."

Kat then got on the bed and tried it out herself.

"You're right," Kat said. "It's a bit small for two people but it is comfortable."

Noble turned and put his arm on Kat. The two cuddled and began closing their eyes. They were finally relaxed enough where they both dozed off.

Chapter 53

There were no sunrises nor were there any sunsets when traveling in space. If one didn't pay attention to the time, one could easily lose track of it. By the time Noble, Blay and Creyson finished all their questions they had for Quanta about the craft, they were almost to the mining station in Uranus.

"We will reach the mining station in sixty minutes," Quanta said.

Creyson volunteered to go out into the mining station and recommended Blay to stay behind to monitor the spacecraft. Blay was more than willing to stay behind since he wasn't too fond of going out into space.

"I like to volunteer to go out there with you," Noble said.

"I could use some assistance," Creyson said. "But I think the rest should stay behind. There's not a lot of room out there."

Kat and Cee-Fu agreed to stay behind. Creyson led Noble to another room in the spacecraft. It was the gear room where all the astronauts' gears were stored. Creyson pointed to a spacesuit and instructed Noble to put them on. It took some time to put all the gears on, but eventually they were both suited up.

"I was assuming the spacesuit was going to be heavier than I thought with all the stuff we had to put on," Noble said.

"They used the latest and lightest materials on all the gears we're wearing," Creyson said. "And the gears are very safe. They've spent thousands of hours testing them."

"That's good to know," Noble said.

"Are you ready?" Creyson asked.

"Yes," Noble answered.

"Then let's go," Creyson said.

Creyson led Noble into another room from the gear room. It was lid brightly. There was nothing in the room except a sitting bench. When the two went inside the room, the door behind them closed and locked.

"This is the launching room for us," Creyson said. "We have to wait until Quanta brings us close to the mining station. The door on that side will open for us and we'll float to the station door and go in. Blay should be able to open the door of the mining station without any issue. Right, Blay?"

"I'm going through the security systems of the mining station," Blay's voice said through an intercom in the launching room. "It looks pretty straight forward. It shouldn't be a problem to unlock the door but I do need you to pull a lever from the outside and inside. I can't do it from here."

"Copy that," Creyson said.

Noble was nervous and excited at the same time. He's never been out in space before although there were space tours where tourists could take to go out into space. But Noble was never excited into going into space because the space tours were just for a few hours and the tourists were just there to experience weightlessness. There was nothing else to do in space, Noble thought.

"We will be arriving to the mining station in five minutes," Quanta said through the intercom.

Creyson went to the wall and grab a hook clamp that was attached to a rope on the wall. He used the hook clamp to hook it into his spacesuit. He could tell Noble was looking at him intently.

"This will ensure we won't float away from Quanta. There's another hook clamp over there," Creyson said as he was pointing to another hook clamp on the other side of the wall.

Noble went and attached the hook clamp to his spacesuit. Both of them saw the mining station getting bigger and bigger through the window as they waited.

"We will reach the mining station in less than one minute," Quanta said through the intercom.

Blay was really impressed with the way Quanta was navigating itself to the mining station. It was getting closer and closer to the mining station's docking door with precision. Blay knew he couldn't get closer like that even if he piloted the spacecraft himself.

Creyson and Noble saw that the mining station's docking door was in sight and they were getting much closer.

"If Quanta can get us within a few feet from the docking door, we may not even need the hooking clamp," Creyson said. "We can just hop into the mining station."

"That would be great," Noble said.

"Hang on, guys. The docking door will be unlocked very soon," Blay said through the intercom.

Quanta was moving so close to the mining station that Creyson and Noble was only about a foot away from the docking door. A moment later, the docking door unlocked thanks to Blay.

"Looks like we're up," Creyson said to Noble.

Noble nodded and then Creyson pushed a button on the wall and the door opened to space. They were both weightless now. Creyson could see the lever by the door of the mining station that Blay was talking about earlier. He grabbed the lever and pulled down on it. The docking door of the mining station opened for them. Creyson used his feet to push off from the floor and hopped through the docking door. Noble followed and did the same thing. They both removed their hooks and hooked them near the front entrance of the door. Moments after that, Creyson pushed a button on the wall of the mining station and the door closed. Creyson then pushed a few more buttons on the wall and oxygen began to fill up the room. A moment later, the monitor on the wall indicated that there was enough oxygen for the astronauts to breath in the facility.

"We can take this off now," Creyson said as he began to take off his helmet.

Noble followed and did exactly what Creyson did.

"Let's go inside," Creyson said as he pushed another button.

The interior door opened, giving them access to the interior of the mining station.

"Okay, we're in," Creyson said into his HIDD. "What do we do next?"

A moment later, Blay's voice came through their HIDDs.

"You have to go to the control room and open the door to the BEAM power supply," Blay said. "There should be another lever in there for that. Quanta should be able to take care of the rest after that."

"Copy that," Creyson said into his HIDD.

Creyson began to walk into the mining station with Noble following closely behind. The two eventually made their way into the control room. Creyson walked over to the control panel and started to push some buttons. He later found the access to opening the door for the BEAM power supply along with the lever on the wall. As soon as Creyson pushed the button and then pulled the lever to open the door for the power supply, an exterior door opened from the outside of the mining station. Blay could see it from the inside of Quanta.

"There it is," Blay said.

Quanta began to move closer to the door for the power supply. When it got close to the door, it opened an exterior door and a claw like device started to appear. It kept getting longer until it reached into the inside of the power area of the mining station. The claw eventually made contact with a latch in the power supply room and locked itself onto the latch.

"I am in place to begin to extract the power pack," Quanta said to Blay. "Shall I begin?"

"Yes," Blay said.

Quanta started to make its calculations.

"It should take about ten minutes," Quanta said.

"Did you guys hear that?" Blay said.

"Loud and clear," Creyson said. "We'll hang around here until Quanta is finished taking the spare power pack."

Noble thought since they had about ten minutes, he wanted to look around the mining station.

"I'm just going to take a look around," Noble said to Creyson.

"Okay, just call me if there's any problems," Creyson said.

"You got it," Noble said and then he walked out of the control room.

A moment later, Noble was able to find the storage room. There was no one around. Noble was able to find the control panel for the room and he touched the screen. He looked at the menu options and then pushed a couple of more buttons. As soon as he was done, a drawer opened. Noble walked to the drawer to see what was in it. When he got there, he was speechless.

There were diamonds and lots of them. These were uncut and unpolished diamonds. But they came from the planet Uranus. Noble knew that Uranus had the temperature and the pressure to produce diamonds in abundance, but it was just a theory. He never knew that it would be a reality since he knew no one had ever brought diamonds back from Uranus. But there they were in the drawer, diamonds from Uranus.

Noble picked a big one in the drawer and looked more closely at it. He then got an idea.

"Blay, can you make it so we can talk in private for a moment?" Noble said into his HIDD.

"Hang on," Blay said as he pushed a few buttons on the control panel. "Okay, no one else can hear us now."

Noble told Blay what he found and what he wanted to do. Blay had to go to the control panel and pushed a few more buttons. A moment later, Blay got his answer.

"Yeah, it could be done," Blay said to Noble.

So Blay instructed Noble on what to do. Noble followed Blay's instructions on what to do as he was pushing some buttons on the control panel in the storage room of the mining station. As soon as Noble finished pushing the buttons, a tiny drawer came out from the wall. Noble went to the tiny drawer and put the diamond that he picked up into the tiny drawer. The tiny drawer then went back into the wall. Noble then walk back to the control panel and pushed another button. Noble was hoping his idea would work.

The extraction of the spare power pack was a success. Quanta was able to move itself back to the docking door to pick up Creyson and Noble. The two were back in the spacecraft about half an hour after the extraction process began. Everyone was glad they were able to pick up an additional power supply for the BEAM Drive.

"So, are we ready to go to Earth 2.0?" Creyson asked.

"Not yet, I just have one more thing I need to do," Noble said.

"What's that?" Kat asked.

"Kat, I love you," Noble said. "I wouldn't have come if you weren't with me. I want us to continue our future journeys together."

"We are and we will," Kat said. "I love you too."

Noble then got down on one knee and took out a diamond from his pocket. It was the diamond that he took earlier but he got it cut and polished thanks to Blay's assistance. The diamond appeared to be two carat, emerald shape. It looked colorless and internally flawless.

"Kat, will you marry me?" Noble asked.

Kat was shocked. There were tears in her eyes.

She then happily said, "Yes, I will marry you."

Chapter 54

The trip to Earth 2.0 was delayed for the next twenty-four hours so Noble and Kat could have a wedding ceremony. Everyone was excited. There was no formal minister to perform the ceremony so Noble asked Cee-Fu if he could do it. Cee-Fu reluctantly said yes knowing there was no other option and he didn't want to disappoint his pupil.

Cee-Fu didn't really know want to do but he made the best of it.

"We have gathered here to celebrate the marriage of Noble and Kat," Cee-Fu began as Noble and Kat stood in front of him, facing each other. "Even though we are in outer space, the sanctity of marriage is universal."

Everyone was smiling.

"Do you, Noble, take Kat as your lawfully wedded wife, to love and to hold, to cherish, for better or worse, until death due you part?" Cee-Fu asked Noble.

"I do," Noble said happily.

"Good," Cee-Fu said. "Do you, Kat, take Noble as your lawfully wedded husband, to love and to hold, to cherish, for better or worse, until death due you part?"

"I do," Kat said emotionally.

"I now pronounce you husband and wife," Cee-Fu said gladly. "You may kiss your bride."

Noble gave Kat a loving and passionate kiss. Blay, Creyson and Cee-Fu all clapped and cheered. Blay then went and hugged Noble and then Kat.

"How are you going to wear your diamond?" Blay asked Kat.

"Here," Kat said as she took out her HIDD and opened a compartment where a few chips could be attached.

The diamond was in the opened slot. It fitted inside the compartment perfectly.

"Now I will have the diamond right on my heart," Kat said as she looked at Noble.

Noble kissed Kat again and then they all headed to the dining area for their meals. Noble and Kat were holding hands as they walked.

The meals were simple and the five enjoyed eating them. They were all in good mood and they had good appetites. Blay then decided to stand up and proposed a toast.

"I've been Noble's best friend since we were teenagers," Blay said. "But ever since he met Kat, he's never been more happy or more in love. I wish you both joy and happiness for the rest of your lives."

Noble got up and went to Blay and gave him a hug.

After dinner, Creyson announced they should all get some rest and then start getting ready for the hibernation process.

"We'll all meet up in the hibernation chamber in ten hours to get ready for our long trip," Creyson said.

Everyone agreed and they left to go back to their bedrooms. Kat went with Noble back to his bedroom.

As soon as Noble and Kat were inside the bedroom, they started to kiss again but more passionately. A moment later, they got on the bed as they were kissing. Kat started to take her clothes off. Noble followed immediately and took his clothes off. The two made love with the view of the stars outside their window.

When everyone woke up, they all got dressed. Noble was glad he was able to make love to Kat before the long trip. He kissed Kat one more time lovingly before they headed out to the main control area. When they got out there, Creyson, Cee-Fu and Blay were already waiting for them.

"I've already programmed Quanta to set a course to Earth 2.0," Creyson said. "We should arrive there in sixty three years, but we'll be asleep for most of the trip."

Noble was holding Kat's hand when he said, "We're ready."

"I'm ready," Cee-Fu said.

Blay nodded and said, "Let's do it."

"Well then, let's go to the hibernation chamber," Creyson said.

They were all staring at the pods inside the hibernation chamber.

"We have to inject more NIBs into our bodies first before we get in," Creyson said.

A robotic arm appeared from the wall with a needle placed at the end.

"These NIBs are programmed to repair our cells and keep us young and alive until we reach our destination," Creyson said as he was pointing to the robotic arm with the needle. "So, who wants to go first?"

Noble raised his hand and volunteered.

"All right, come on up then," Creyson said.

Noble walked up to Creyson.

"I'll need your shoulder," Creyson said..

Noble took his outfit off to expose his shoulder for Creyson.

"It's going to hurt a bit," Creyson warned Noble as he stuck the needle into Noble's shoulder. He then injected the liquid into Noble's shoulder.

Noble felt the sting of the needle and he felt pain when the liquid was being injected into him. There was more pain than he expected, but it wasn't a horrible experience.

Kat went next. She didn't like the pain, but she endured it. Blay then got the shot followed by Cee-Fu. Creyson was the last one to get the injection and he did it himself. Afterward, he disposed the syringes and the empty vials into a bin.

"Quanta, prepare five pods for hibernation," Creyson said.

"Hibernation confirmed for five pods," Quanta said.

A moment later, doors for five of the pods opened. Creyson didn't say anything and got into one of the pods. Noble and Kat picked two pods that were next to each other. They kissed one more time and then they got in.

"I'll see you soon," Noble said.

"I love you," Kat said.

"I love you too," Noble said.

Blay and Cee-Fu both got into their respective pods.

"Hopefully we'll still look decent sixty three years later," Blay said.

Everyone smiled and thought that was pretty funny.

"Is everyone ready?" Creyson asked.

Everyone said they were.

"Quanta, commence the hibernation process," Creyson said.

"Hibernation commencing," Quanta said.

A moment later, the five doors on the pods began to close. Everyone was nervous but they knew they would be safe. Soon, all of them began to close their eyes. Chemicals were being injected into their pods to induce sleep. The five fell asleep a couple of minutes later.

A robotic arm came out from the inside of each of the pods. It got close to the left arm of each person. It then injected a small plastic tube into their arms. Liquid then began to flow into the arm. It was the way Quanta regulated their body fluid levels. The robotic arms then moved to their lower abdomen area, below their belly buttons. Each robotic arm then injected two other plastic tubes into their bodies. Liquid then began to come out through the tubes. Those tubes were used to extract body waste.

Quanta then began to lower the temperature inside the pods. It needed to lower the body temperature by ten degrees so it could slow down the body's metabolic rate. It needed to do this slowly to avoid any adverse reaction from the body. After about two hours later, the body temperature was ten degrees lower on all five of the passengers. They were officially in hibernation state.

Quanta was programmed to go to Earth 2.0. It proceeded to turn off all unnecessary power and began to speed up close to the speed of light. It took the spacecraft another twenty four hours later but it finally reached 99.9% of light speed. With Quanta navigating the spacecraft, the five were on their way to Earth 2.0.

Chapter 55

A vehicle was approaching to a large house in a remote part of the state of Montana. The house was big and there was no other house visible nearby. The vehicle stopped in front of the house and the door opened automatically. An older man and a young woman got out of the vehicle.

"So this is our new home," the older man said as his voice sounded just like Hunter.

"We'll use this house as our new base for our movement," the young woman said as her voice sounded just like Jumma.

A moment later, Slade's head popped out from the vehicle.

"This is what your package got you," Slade said. "It's the best package available. There is a vehicle in the garage. This is what you requested, right?"

Hunter turned to Slade and nodded with satisfaction.

"Then this concludes our business transaction," Slade said. "Good luck to you."

Slade's head popped back into the vehicle and the door closed automatically. A moment later, the vehicle drove off. Hunter looked at the vehicle until it disappeared. He took a deep breath and exhaled. There was a look of melancholy in his expression that Jumma could tell on her father's face.

"Come on, Dad," Jumma said as she took her father's hand. She gave him a look of confidence as if she was telling him that everything would be okay.

Hunter looked back at Jumma and nodded. It all seemed surreal to him. The two then proceeded to walk to the house. They paused for a moment when they got to the front door. They then went into the house and the front door closed behind them.

Chapter 56

Back in Atlantic City, a large group of agents led by Director Proc were inside the launch station. There were agents walking everywhere gathering evidence on what happened. Director Proc was in the station's control room, looking at the computer screens on the wall while three of his agents were sitting down, controlling the computers to the screens. There were engineers and scientists that worked at the station standing behind Director Proc.

One of the agents that were sitting down by the control monitor was typing something and then said, "Sir, it looks like they're heading for Earth 2.0."

Director Proc thought it would be fourteen hundred years later in Earth's time by the time they reached that planet. The five were no threat to the Agency anymore, he thought. But to be sure, Director Proc ordered his agents to pull all the files Creyson was working on in the last few months.

One of the agents by the computers pulled the files up onto the screen. It looked like Creyson was winding down his cases in preparation for the trip in space. He didn't have any cases in the past ten days except the recent assignment of finding the file for the

Agency. Director Proc didn't think there was anything to worry about with Creyson being gone.

"Let me see what Blay was working on," Director Proc said.

A moment later, Blay's files were up on the screens. Director Proc saw how Blay was working to get the restricted files from COZ. Blay wasn't working on anything else except that during the last few months. Director Proc already knew about the hacking Blay was doing and didn't think that was a threat anymore.

"Now pull up the files for Noble," Director Proc ordered.

When the agent pulled up Noble's files, the screens showed full of complex math formulas. Director Proc looked at the formulas with intense interest. But the more he looked into the math formulas, the more concerned he became.

"My my," Director Proc said and then turned around to the scientists and engineers. "How soon can you make another spacecraft so we can go after them? But I want this one to carry a battalion of agents, because apparently a dozen or so agents can't stop them."

The engineers and scientists all looked puzzled.

The lead engineer thought about it and then said, "Maybe two years."

"You have one year to complete it," Director Proc said. "The Agency will provide you with everything to make it happen."

Director Proc was about to walk out of the room when an agent asked him a question.

"Sir, why are we going after them when they don't appear to be a threat to us anymore?" The agent asked.

Director Proc paused a moment and then said, "Because it looks like Noble is close to solving it."

The agent didn't understand and then asked, "What is he close to solving, sir?"

Director Proc then looked at the screen and said, "Everything."

Chapter 57

The space ride to Earth 2.0 was smooth and uneventful. The five passengers were still in hibernation after sixty three years. The ETA to Earth 2.0 was still about a week away, but Quanta decided to begin ending their hibernation so their bodies could get acclimated back to normal. So Quanta began by increasing their body temperature back to normal. A couple of hours later, the body temperature for all five were back to normal. Quanta then removed the plastic tubes from their bodies. The pods were slowly being filled with a chemical to induce the passengers to wake up.

Noble began to open his eyes slowly. Everything looked blurry and he felt really groggy. Every muscle in his body ached. He had a hard time moving. He needed more time to wake up. But he could hear the pod door opening, but he still couldn't move his body yet. His body ached all over. Everything looked so bright and blurry still. He had a hard time seeing anything clearly. He felt his tongue being really dried in his mouth.

It took a few more minutes before the vision in Noble's eyes started to get back into focus. His body still ached all over but he could start moving his fingers. He then began to move his head to look around. It was still very bright for his eyes. He couldn't see anything except the side walls of the hibernation pod that he was in. So he made an attempt to get up. It was much harder than he thought because his body was so stiff from sleeping for so long. But he did it anyway and eventually got into the sitting position inside his pod. He looked around and noticed Kat sitting up and looking groggy. He then saw Blay, Cee-Fu and Creyson waking up. They were in the same condition as he was.

"Kat, are you okay?" Noble asked.

"Yeah, no one said waking up from this was going to be this rough," Kat said groggily.

"It's going to take a few days for us to get back to our usual self," Creyson said. "But I'm glad we all woke up safely."

"Please tell me I don't look so old that I can't even recognize myself," Blay said.

Noble looked at Blay and then said, "No, you look just as ugly as the last time I saw you."

Everyone laughed.

"Very funny," Blay said. "After sleeping for sixty three years, you still have jokes as soon as you wake up."

Creyson looked and noticed everyone didn't age at all. The hibernation process worked, he thought.

"We should all go to the medical room to get a full exam to be sure that everyone is fine," Creyson said. "So as soon as you can, follow me."

The medical room looked like a modern medical facility. There were three medical pods similar to the ones used in hibernation but these were smaller, sleeker and made mostly out of glass. Noble, Kat and Blay were in the medical pods getting their exams. Images of their internal organs were appearing in the monitor screens. The scan didn't show any anomalies. A needle from each of the pods came out from the side walls and injected it into their arms to extract a blood sample.

"Everything looks good," Creyson said. "The results show the three of you aged about a year and a half. It's better than I expected."

"Thanks, but it feels funny that after sixty three years that we spent sleeping in a pod that as soon as we wake up, we're back in a pod," Noble said jokingly.

"My body is sore all over," Blay said.

"You three can come out from there and relax a bit," Creyson said. "Cee-Fu and I will get our exams next."

Creyson and Cee-Fu went next and the results were the same as the previous three.

"Did we make it to Earth 2.0?" Cee-Fu asked when he and Creyson got out of the medical pods.

"Quanta is showing we're about a week away," Creyson said. "It woke us up early so that we can get our bodies back to normal."

"I'm going to need more than a week to recuperate," Blay said.

"There are a lot of stretching exercises we can do to get our bodies back into shape," Creyson said.

"But before we do that, how about we eat something?" Noble asked happily. "I hadn't eaten any food in sixty three years. I'm starving."

Creyson laughed and said, "You're right. Let's go get some food from the dining area."

Everyone had a good appetite while eating their food. Noble still couldn't believe he had been asleep for sixty three years. What's even more shocking for Noble was that it was now fourteen hundred years later on Earth. Things must have advanced dramatically since the last time he was there, Noble thought. But he couldn't think too much about that because he had to get himself ready for the new planet, his new home. He was so glad that Kat was fine and that she was with him on the journey.

Things were back to fairly normal a week later. Quanta was slowing down the spacecraft because it was getting close to Earth 2.0. The muscle soreness and body aches were virtually gone from the five passengers. Creyson showed the others stretching exercises to help with the muscle soreness. Cee-Fu showed the others some Tai-Chi moves which he claimed would also help with the muscle soreness.

What little muscle soreness that was left in the bodies of the passengers disappeared as soon as Earth 2.0 was in their sight through the window.

"There it is," Creyson said. "Earth 2.0."

Noble looked at the planet with amazement and said, "Our new home."

"Can we just call it New Earth instead of Earth 2.0?" Kat asked. "I think New Earth sounds better."

"New Earth. I like it," Cee-Fu said.

"When can we go down there?" Blay asked.

"First, we have to get close to the planet so we can orbit around it," Creyson said. "We then send a probe into the planet to measure the temperature and radiation levels on the planet and to take samples of the air, water and soil. We have to analyze them to see if it's habitable for us. The probe will also take pictures and videos so we have an idea of what the planet looks like."

"Let's hope it is habitable for us," Noble said.

"I hope so too," Creyson said.

As Quanta got close to New Earth and orbited around the planet, the five could see the planet looked very much like Earth. It had a large land mass and an ocean. There were clouds in the atmosphere like Earth. The land mass itself looked mostly green. That was good news for everyone because the green color would represent vegetation, trees, grass, leaves and other possible plant life.

"Quanta, send a probe into the planet to determine habitability for us," Creyson said.

"Request acknowledged," Quanta said. "Probe One will be sent in one minute."

A minute later, a small probe ejected out of one of Quanta's outer doors and was heading into New Earth. The five could see the probe flying into the new planet and disappeared into its atmosphere.

"Now we wait for the result," Creyson said.

Noble and Kat were holding hands and paced around the spacecraft. They were too excited and nervous to be sitting down while waiting for the result. Blay was by the control screen hoping the result would appear right away. Cee-Fu kept himself busy by doing some Tai-Chi exercises. Creyson was by the window, admiring the view of the new planet.

A couple of hours later, Blay was getting nervous. Probe One should have responded by now, he thought.

"What's taking it so long?" Blay asked Creyson.

But before Creyson could say anything, the results from Probe One began to display on the screen.

"It's here! We have it!" Blay yelled.

Everyone rushed to the screens to take a look.

"No harmful radiation, temperature at 75 degrees Fahrenheit, air quality is better than Earth, clean drinking water in the river and soil sample is primed for agriculture," Creyson said happily.

"But look at the gravity on the planet," Blay said. "It's more than our earth."

"That's expected," Creyson said. "The planet is bigger than our Earth so we were assuming the gravity would be heavier."

"So it'll be tough to move around?" Kat asked.

"At first, but we can program our NIBs to adjust our muscles to compensate for the extra gravity on the planet," Creyson said. "But we can experience the gravity first and then see if we need the NIBs to do that for us."

The next thing appeared were photos of the new planet. The five were looking at them excitedly. The sky was blue. The grass was green. There was a river running through the land. But there was a large part of the land that was covered with thick forest. There were even some birds flying above the forest.

Noble saw the birds and thought that was amazing. He just saw photos of animals from a different planet. So life does exist in another planet, he thought. The planet's evolution process was similar to earth's for birds, Noble concluded..

"Are there any hostile animals down there?" Noble asked.

"The probe only noticed the birds and they don't appear to be a threat," Creyson said. "And it couldn't get a good read in the forest because there's too much interference."

"So when do we go down there?" Blay asked.

"Now sounds good," Creyson replied.

Chapter 58

It was a warm and sunny day. Quanta was parked on a field of grass overlooking a river to one side and beautiful hills with big trees on the other side of the land. It's been a week since the five landed on New Earth and they've been enjoying every minute of it. They've only explored a few square miles of the new planet. They figured they had the rest of their lives to explore the rest of the area on this planet. There were only five of them and it's a huge planet. Besides, beyond the hills were thick forests. Creyson warned that if one wasn't careful, one would get lost in the forest very quickly. So everyone decided to stay close to Quanta and would not venture beyond the hills.

On this day, a couple of droids from the spacecraft was on the land to cultivate and to plant the seeds in the land so they could start growing some vegetables. Quanta was stored with lots of plant seeds. Everyone decided it was a good idea to start growing their own harvest before they start running out of food.

Blay decided to take a swim in the river. The water was clean and warm. He hadn't been this relaxed in a long time. He still couldn't believe he was on a different planet. They really got lucky finding this planet to be habitable.

Cee-Fu was about a hundred yards in front of Quanta. He was sparring with Kat because she wanted to learn martial arts like Noble and Blay. They were fighting in Wing Chun style and Kat was learning rapidly. But Cee-Fu didn't think she was ready yet. She still had much to learn, he thought. They stopped and he suggested she take a break. Kat walked to a nearby area and sat down to take her break.

Meanwhile, Cee-Fu picked up a fighting staff to exercise and to practice some martial art moves. His movements were so fluid, like a dancer in a ballet, Creyson thought as he was looking at Cee-Fu. Creyson then decided to walk up to Cee-Fu.

"I really admire your fighting style," Creyson said to Cee-Fu.

"I am a fan of yours too," Cee-Fu said.

"Would you care to spar with me?" Creyson said.

"It would be an honor," Cee-Fu said.

Creyson then picked up a fighting staff on the ground. He moved it around to test the weight of the staff. It had good even weight to it. The two men then bowed to each other.

Cee-Fu bent his knees slightly and as soon as he did that, Creyson charged right at him. Kat heard the noise and turned around and saw what was happening. Blay heard the noise too and saw Cee-Fu and Creyson fighting. He rushed back to take a closer look. The two were evenly matched in their fighting skills until a victor prevailed moments later.

But what the two men didn't know was that a few hundred yards away in the dense forest, someone was watching the two of them fight. The forest covered the view of that someone. But he looked at his own left hand. He had five fingers just like them only that his hand was covered in short brown fur. His forearm was bigger and more muscular than them, he thought. The forearm was covered in short brown fur as well. He was amazed at how the two creatures he had never seen before in his life were fighting using their wooden staffs. Then he looked at his own right hand and saw he too was holding a fighting staff very similar to the two creatures fighting. The amazing thing was that his fighting technique was similar to theirs. He would guess he could beat the two creatures if he had to. But the leaves in the forest covered the view of this observer. His face was not visible. The only thing that was visible on the face was one of the observer's brown eyes. There was short brown fur around the eye as well. A moment later, the observer disappeared from view.

Chapter 59

Noble wasn't aware of the fighting. He went to one of the hills that were closed to the edge of the forest. He sat down by one of the big trees, the nicest one he could find. There he sat and realized how lucky they were in finding this planet to be a new home for them. He enjoyed the view so much that it really reminded him of his home planet, Earth.

Then something got Noble thinking. He began to realize that there were many similarities between this planet and Earth. He then concluded that nothing happens by chance. So he tapped his HIDD and pulled out his math formulas. He then started to read just his formulas and did it at a rapid pace. After ten minutes had gone by, he stopped.

"Oh my god!" he yelled out loud.

Noble then got up and began running back to Quanta.

The fight was over between Cee-Fu and Creyson with no one getting hurt. The two were having tea with Blay and Kat when Noble rushed into the spacecraft. He was out of breath.

Kat looked at Noble and said, "Noble, did you see Cee-Fu and Creyson were sparring earlier and …hey, what's wrong?"

Kat saw Noble was trying to say something but he was out of breath. So she got up and went over to him. The other three got up and looked at Noble with concern.

Noble was trying to speak but couldn't. He was still out of breath.

Cee-Fu gave Noble a cup of tea and said, "Drink this and relax... breath."

Noble took a sip of the tea and that seemed to do the trick. He was able to calm down after a couple of minutes.

"So what's wrong?" Kat asked.

"Nothing's wrong," Noble said happily. "Everything is great!"

"Why are you out of breath?" Kat asked.

"Because I think I solved it," Noble said.

"You solved what?" Kat asked.

"The theory," Noble said.

"What theory?" Kat asked.

"The theory of everything," Noble said. "I know how our universe got created."

"It is common knowledge that The Big Bang created our universe," Blay said.

"But I know what created The Big Bang," Noble said.

The four were very interested at that point.

"Please tell us, Noble," Cee-Fu said.

Noble paused for a moment and then said, "You should all sit down for this."